CW00493548

About the Author

Nick Love is a former Royal Marine Commando, who also served in the Falklands in 1982; he retired in 1987. The book is set in his beautiful home city. He came up with the plot whilst training daily for the 2015 London Marathon, running around the leafy lanes of Lincolnshire. He is a 59-year-old who, as a person with dyslexia, has written this book in a no-nonsense way which he finds enjoyable and easy to read. This journey has not been easy for him, but he believes the result paints a nice mental picture for the reader, in deliberate bite-size chapters.

2,600 Feet per Second

Nick Love

2,600 Feet per Second

Olympia Publishers
London

www.olympiapublishers.com
OLYMPIA PAPERBACK EDITION

Copyright © Nick Love 2023

The right of Nick Love to be identified as author of
this work has been asserted in accordance with sections 77 and 78 of
the Copyright, Designs and Patents Act 1988.

All Rights Reserved

No reproduction, copy or transmission of this publication
may be made without written permission.
No paragraph of this publication may be reproduced,
copied or transmitted save with the written permission of the publisher,
or in accordance with the provisions
of the Copyright Act 1956 (as amended).

Any person who commits any unauthorised act in relation to
this publication may be liable to criminal
prosecution and civil claims for damage.

A CIP catalogue record for this title is
available from the British Library.

ISBN: 978-1-80074-742-5

This is a work of fiction.
Names, characters, places and incidents originate from the writer's
imagination. Any resemblance to actual persons, living or dead, is
purely coincidental.

First Published in 2023

Olympia Publishers
Tallis House
2 Tallis Street
London
EC4Y 0AB

Printed in Great Britain

Dedication

This book is dedicated to everyone who has overcome their own adversities with courage and strength.

Acknowledgements

Thank you to my beautiful wife, Delia (just one more page), and my old friends, Ian Jamieson and Steve Sefton for helping me believe in myself and this novel.

Prologue

Beem lay cold, wet, and hungry, dressed head to foot in his handmade, well-worn, overused ghillie suit. He was looking directly at his prey through the powerful 5-25 x 56 Schmidt & Bender telescopic sight, which was sitting on top of his hand-built weapon, the Accuracy International Arctic Warfare bolt-action, and deadly L96A1 sniper rifle prototype. He felt, what would seem strange to most, a strong connection to his weapon. It had been his guardian and he had been its for so long now, it was like any long-term relationship, comforting just to be together. As he crawled noiselessly to his final position, he contemplated how he had come to be in this place at this time, to do this job. He realised it had been a culmination of the thousands of hours spent at hundreds of rifle ranges, honing his God-given natural talent, combined with his ability to spend long weeks alone in splendid isolation, never needing the company of others. This meant his mind never wandered and he never felt the pangs of loneliness – a rare gift which was very much appreciated in his chosen profession. It was a gift born and nurtured through growing up as an abandoned, but resilient child who was ultimately free from normal constraints and boundaries. This allowed him to develop skills which would be invaluable in his chosen life.

Then came the much desired, even greatly anticipated, but rarely achieved solo missions. Most operational snipers worked normally in a team of two as a minimum or a maximum of three

– a spotter, normally a must-have; and a dogsbody, a nice-to-have. Only a handful of snipers across the globe could or would perform solo. His missions grew rapidly in complexity and were performed across differing landscapes. They spanned every terrain, of every combat arena, which those intelligent men leading from behind mahogany desks could think of. Those who had chosen to make war in once beautiful landscapes, marring them forever. Still, ours is not to reason why and all that!

While he lay there in the unforgiving cold, hard mud, it was only then that Chris began to realise that conflict, in all its guises, was something he had grown tired of. Like many veterans who had seen combat first-hand, he knew the futility of those enterprises. *Ours not to reason why, ours but to do and* [try not to] *die.*

Bracing himself for his assigned task, he settled into the prone shooting position, whilst making sure his lead foot was firmly anchored in place. He felt the fleeting cacophony of his battle-weary thoughts begin to evaporate, like wafts of smoke on the cool Antarctic breeze, just as quickly as they had formed. He slowly allowed his surroundings to dissolve, detaching him from the biting cold and clawing mud, letting his keen, animal-like senses dull to the point he could no longer feel the wind relentlessly tugging at his ghillie suit or feel the constant hunger pains, which danced across his ribcage. His emotions and personal welfare in check, he was no longer worried about the cold nibbling at his every exposed part, and the worry of frostbite became a distant memory. He was entering, for want of a better term, the zone! The zone was a euphemistic term for that place which allowed one human to kill another human without hesitation or remorse, even in defence of the realm and the people of the Falkland Islands. He had fine-tuned getting to and staying in the zone through years of personal, practical experience, although to look at his baby face complexion and natural jet-black, crew-cut hair, you could be forgiven for assuming this was his very first time and not, as it turned out, his last. With total clarity and deliberate care, his breathing was slowing, becoming more rhythmically controlled. A natural pause of two to three seconds occurs between each respiratory cycle. Now he extended that pause to ten to fifteen seconds, allowing his breathing muscles to relax and settle to their natural point of aim. Even though he had been stalking his prey for over six hours, since daybreak, this was the first vantage point which had offered a clear, though still difficult, long-range shot. He had taken his time to get close for this kill shot because he always wanted, when possible, to use the eye socket as an entry point for headshots, even if it meant extra days of stalking. The bonus of the extra time taken meant he really got to know his prey: he was able to note important quirks, twitches or tics all gleaned from the hour upon hour of particular observations, all whilst remaining totally stationary in the prone, ready to fire position. Experience had taught him a valuable lesson – to always trust the biology of a human head. You could add nothing bulletproof to an eye which would protect it from a single well-aimed shot. It was funny the memories that competed for space, especially while he was trying to clear his mind. Now, in his own mind's eye, he remembered an experience with such clarity, it could have been a film he was watching; it was to be one of many valuable lessons learnt. Whilst in Northern Ireland, during the height of the troubles, he had shot a target in the back of the head, only for the bullet to lodge ineffectively into a titanium plate. The IRA lieutenant had been fitted with this as a result of a homemade rucksack bomb being prematurely detonated mid-carry. The resulting explosion had nearly blown his own head off! So, he had been a lucky bugger twice! But, a month later, Chris had made sure there would be no third time lucky.

He knew lessons like these only came with active service experience, hence why he had been selected for this mission. He was, therefore, as determined as ever to make that experience count and succeed once again, against even the highest of odds. So, just to be one hundred and that impossible ten per cent sure, it would be instant death, a clean kill. There would be no need for a time-consuming confirmation look through his scope, no second shot required, no hanging around to get spotted or caught, and no room for error. This was just too important, not just for him, but for every combatant and civilian, regardless of nationality.

At last, all known factors were taken into consideration: wind, precipitation, air temperature, cloud movement, terrain, type of grass, range deflection, bullet speed angle reduction ratio, fixed obstacles, target characteristics, magnetic forces, wildlife, gravity, sunbeams, rainbows, birdsong, insect farts – the lot!

Well, today had it all: a blustery wind veering between NNE to NNW at 11 knots, according to his portable wind gauge; drizzly rain at a 23 degree angle from the east at 8 knots; intermittent sunbeams peeking through a low, fast-moving nimbus cloud cover; boggy methane-popping terrain with the occasional large lake of haze producing frozen water which, at 2 degrees Celsius, was cold heading towards freezing; plus the 658 metres between him and his prey – only half the full range for this weapon, but because it was a high value, high ranking target, he had stalked closer than was essential. This was still going to be a difficult shot and he was running out of time. He had been given a three-day window for this operation to succeed and had been stalking the General for two and a half days over the weekend already. The forward recce troop intel, in connection with the combined SBS and SAS (for once working together) observations gathered directly from the Argentine capital, had correctly shown him arriving with his young daughter, either to show off his daughter to his troops or his troops to his daughter! Either way, it confirmed he had the power and the control. I mean, who else would have the arrogance to bring a teenage dependant on a live battlefield visit, even with the protection of the battle-hardened 601 Battalion. The same intelligence had him bugging out in just two hours, back to Buenos Aires. While there, he was to head up the military junta, and the General was going to be good at that! Thanks to the ruthlessness with which he had taken control of the armed forces and the banks, the coup d'état had given him total power, which meant he now had a hold on the army and the people alike. He had his foot on their throat and he was going to make sure he kept it there. Once he was gone from this South Atlantic Island, he would be forever off the radar, out of play. This would be the last chance to end this conflict quickly – cut the head off the serpent, kill the body, break the soul, and lose the will.

The mainly conscripted Argentinean Army had taken some very heavy losses already in the conflict to gain sovereignty over what they called the Malvinas in the last nine weeks. Nevertheless, the feared 601 Battalion were gaining momentum, inner strength and confidence almost daily. Only the killing of the General would spell the end of the Falkland's war, therefore, saving many lives from the invading Argentinians, along with the defending mixed British services armed forces. More importantly for Captain Christopher (Laser) Beem, this would be his last detachment from his family in the M&AW Cadre, and his last ever operational mission for 42 Commando Royal Marines or any other fighting force, here and now on 14 June 1982 at 11:55 Zulu, twelve years, thirty-four days, six hours, and fifty-five minutes after joining the elite corps as a spotty-faced Junior Marine. A naive boy barely out of school, he had loved the Marines, and in turn, they had loved him back, giving him rank, respect, responsibility and an unshakable comradeship, which few would ever feel or could ever understand. There was a bond which was as unwavering as he had to be now, accordingly with all that service and history behind him. Once he was done, it was contract up, time to leave, relax, and be a civvy.

But here, now, he finally took a steady aim. No more distractions, no more introspective thoughts, which are best left deep in the hardly ever visited memory bank, while the valuable seconds ticked by. He had a job to do, and one he was good at.

Chris took up the first stage of the trigger, his finger as steady as ever. He squeezed gently, despite having no feeling in any of his fingers, them being so completely numbed by the Antarctic-level cold. He applied even more gentle but steady pressure with just the right amount of kinetic energy. His aim was accurately adjusted. His body and sharp mind could now meet and reach a perfect balance, in tune with nature, serene, sovereign, with a beat of its own, every movement foreseen, conceived, rehearsed to the very last detail, so that when the time is right, when the fickleness of the elements have been factored in and the absolute focus of the mind is instilled in every part of the body, that one shot is released, and it takes but one instance, at one with every beat of nature, able to take into account all the known factors, and even some unknown ones. From his now completely unobstructed and totally unobserved view over the 658 metre distance, and with an almost imperceptible movement, at a natural respiratory pause, he confidently completed the action, which was driven by passion and bound by perfection. He fired at 2,600 feet per second.

Chapter One

Beem lay warm, hungry, and motionless in his marital bed, unusually warm for once because he still had covers on him, and motionless because it was 6 a.m. on the day of his wife Sophie's birthday.

He was forgoing his routine six-mile run so he would be able to make her breakfast in bed. Not that Sophie would appreciate it; she disliked anyone making a fuss over her, always embarrassed to be the centre of attention, despite this being such an intimate gathering.

Chris crept out of the room on tiptoes and headed to Tilly's bedroom. He paused at the door, which had a new hand-painted sign which simply said Matilda's Room. It had a small hand-drawn unicorn in pink, although Chris doubted that unicorns were actually pink in real life! It was the name change which told him she was growing up fast, way too fast for his liking.

He lightly tapped on the door with the ends of his fingers, holding his breath, half hoping she would still be asleep; it would be quicker without her 'help' in the kitchen.

The thought made him smile. He really loved every fibre of his beautiful daughter, as he did his fantastic wife, but sometimes he needed his own space to manoeuvre, especially in the mornings. Hence, the daily run, clearing his mind and steeling him for the challenges of the day, both internal and external. The external challenges, mainly due to the recession, were beginning to cause more stress and worry for him, much more than was usual.

Enough of that. Today was for celebration and that was all.

On the second gentle tap, Tilly burst through the door like a sleepy whirling dervish, a cyclone with bad breath and sleep-encrusted eyes.

'Morning, Dad!' was all she could muster before she headed straight to the bathroom.

Bugger! thought Chris. He had planned to get in there ahead of her, especially today. There was a lot to do before Sophie awoke and he knew Tilly always took ages, like her mum. Do not ever get in a queue behind them both – it was like time stood still.

"Please do not be too long, beautiful! You know we've got to get a wiggle on, Tilly. Tilly! Can you hear me?" he whispered.

Rushing out of the bathroom, banging the door against him as she did so, she had heard him, the look on her face told him that. She only said, "I know, Dad," and marched back to her room, presumably to get dressed. Well, that's what he hoped.

Once they were both downstairs, they set about making the birthday breakfast. Bacon, eggs, sausages (plain pork, Sophie didn't like his favourite Lincolnshire type), tomatoes, beans, mushrooms, hash browns and buttered toast – an Olympic breakfast by any standard. He was always amazed someone so petite, with such a small frame, could eat that amount of food in one sitting and not put an ounce of weight on, the lucky girl. His lucky girl. He smiled.

"Dad," asked Tilly. "What did you do with Mum's present?" He had hidden it in his 'man cave'. Well, it was just a plain old garden shed, in reality. But a boy could dream.

He dashed out to get it because he did not want Tilly's prying eyes there. At least one hiding place had to remain secret. The present, from them both, was a stunning 24ct gold cross on an

18ct gold belcher chain. It had cost more than he could afford at this time, but he wasn't going to admit that. Ever.

"Here you go, Tilly," he said, handing her the present. He could not help but have a sense of pride in what a thoughtful young lady she had become, saving all her own birthday and Christmas money to be able to contribute. She had, of course, been pleased when he had returned it.

"Dad!" Tilly retorted, a rebuff for using her little girl's name, now at twelve years old, she wanted her more grown-up full Christian name. But she still smiled – she liked him calling her that really.

"*M.A... T.I.L... D.A*," he sarcastically spelt out, smiling, and they both laughed out loud. "Shush!" he whispered, and they both laughed again, then got on with the task in hand.

Orange juice, tea (NATO standard), two sugars and lots of milk.

Tilly finished the birthday card, the one she had started last week. She was a bit of a perfectionist and had made four cards prior to this one, so Chris was grateful that this one had turned out precisely as she had wanted. He had to admit she had an eye for detail.

She grabbed her recorder. "Ready, Dad?" she whispered, giggling just a little.

They silently made their way back up the stairs and into the master bedroom, which was still in darkness. Well, it was only 7.30 a.m.

Chris flicked the light on, while Tilly played *Happy Birthday* on her recorder, to a now fully awake and sitting bolt upright in bed Sophie.

"Oh, you're awake," said Matilda, somewhat crestfallen, even surprised.

"Of course. You made enough noise to wake the dead." Sophie smiled.

"Sorry. Happy Birthday, beautiful." Chris placed the tray on her lap, spilling the orange juice a little in the process. "Oops!" He gave a sheepish grin.

They all sat on the bed while Sophie opened her professionally wrapped present – Tilly was particularly good at that. Well, she was particularly good at most things.

"Oh, my darlings, you really shouldn't have. It's just too much," Sophie scolded him for his extravagance, whilst making no attempt to disguise the delight she felt for the gift.

She kissed them both, spilling the orange juice just a little bit more.

They talked while Sophie polished off the entire breakfast, admired the cross and chain, and discussed what they each would be doing for the rest of that day. As it was a Monday, obviously a school/workday, then not a lot was planned. They all agreed they were looking forward to dinner out, for a change.

The girls were, for once, quick to use the bathroom and ready themselves for the day ahead. Then, in a flash, they were gone. This suited Chris. He was looking into the option of arranging a small loan. Re(re)mortgaging yet again was out of the question, so it was going to be a personal, unsecured one, and they came at a price. His mood dipped as he was forced back into reality and at having to face up to his near-daily recession-driven financial worries, once again.

It had taken the better part of the day but, with considerable relief, he had managed to secure a lifeline, allowing his usual happy family man mode to return, thankfully long before his girls arrived home for the evening.

The happy contented family man was his default position; it

came easily to him, with such a wonderful family. He basked in the warmth they radiated. He knew it was a cliché, but he also knew it was true – he really did enjoy a seemingly rare, happy, stable marriage. He had worked hard to make sure it stayed that way, despite his best efforts to derail it from time to time. It was only the recent, relatively long-lasting deterioration in his business, resulting in a few dark clouds on his horizon, which put a damper on it, not that his much-beloved family would ever know or even suspect how bad it was becoming. He had always known how to play his cards close to his chest when it was required. Like now.

This evening, they had been to the fabulous White Hart Hotel, an old fourteenth century coaching inn, now a modern five-star hotel, with a magnificent restaurant, a three-minute walk from Lincoln Castle and Cathedral and ten minutes from his home. It was fit for a queen, with royal prices to match.

The meal had been sumptuous, the courses and the wine flowed, and they had laughed and laughed until they had cried.

Now he lay in his warm cosy bed, in their warm cosy house, with their warm cosy life, and considered all was well with the world.

He was a lucky man, and he knew it. He just hoped his luck would hold out long enough to let him ride out this fiscal storm. They would be fine. Of that, he was sure.

Little did he know…

Chapter Two

One week later, Beem lay cold, hungry, and motionless in his marital bed. Cold because Sophie, his wife of seventeen years, always wanted the window wide open, mainly due to her early onset of menopause. In a bizarre nightly ritual, she would first fling the duvet off her side of the bed, covering Chris in the process, whereupon he became overheated and wide awake. Then she would secure up to eighty per cent of the bed as she lay there in a weird starfish pose, occasionally slapping him in the face for good measure. Then, in what seemed like just a minute later, she would pull all of the duvets, including his half, back over her until she was cocooned and snug as a bug, as it were. This relatively new, totally unconscious act of duvet sabotage meant Chris was often frozen out. This morning, he felt frozen out for a different reason – his usually happy marriage had hit a stormy patch. It had been building for over a year and was slowly transforming into a full-blown tempest. Last night's row had been a frightening experience for both of them; only the appearance of Tilly had stopped them coming to blows, metaphorically, not physically, but verbal blows hurt just as much, didn't they?

He started his morning routine pretty much the same every day – weather, holidays, and unbreakable commitments allowing – as he had done for the last twenty-three years or so. He got up around 6 a.m., did the usual ablutions, and kissed Sophie's sleeping forehead. He moved a lock of her auburn hair from her pretty oval face, with her perfect button of a nose, jade green eyes and almond skin, hoping it would rub away the hurtful words from last night. He headed down the hall to look in on Tilly, who had fortunately inherited her mother's good looks. She was mature beyond her years, and even at the tender age of just twelve years old, she was emulating her mother's mannerisms – cocking her head to the left whilst listening wholeheartedly to whoever was speaking to her, thus giving them her undivided attention and making them feel all the more special for it. He was the only person who could get away with calling her that now, although he used it sparingly, in her presence at least.

He lovingly looked at her sleeping form and despite a few remaining clouds of sadness hanging over him from last night's argument, he couldn't help but be reminded of how lucky he was to have a beautiful twelve-year-old daughter. It didn't seem so long ago that both he and Sophie thought that, after suffering several miscarriages, the blessing of a child may never happen. That heartache was still there in the recesses of his mind, even though Tilly was here, present and all correct, ruling their lives. He still, after all this time, felt the need to occasionally take himself away from the eyes of the world, where he would deliberately relive the memories. Like picking at a scab, it often brought him to the edge of tears, but that was okay. It wasn't just for the painful losses; it was also for all he had gained.

After a quick look and with 'do not disturb' in mind, he headed down the well-trodden staircase of their early Victorian-era cottage. It was situated in a quiet uphill section of the city of Lincoln's historic core, near the castle and cathedral but not so close to the frequent peeling of the bells which disturbed the idyllic setting.

Once downstairs and sitting in his office-cum-work room, cum-personal storage cupboard, he dressed in his familiar Nike running top and Ron Hill tracksters, something he had done for nearly all his adult life. He had a selection of running shoes to choose from, and he always had three or four pairs on the go; ones which had done a marathon, used for long road work; ones for cross-country, the dirty smelly ones that Sophie was always trying to bin; and a brand-new pair of ASICS GEL-Cumulus II, ready to be broken in for this year's Great North Run in Newcastle, one of his favourite half marathons.

This morning, it was the turn of the smelly pair, as it had rained in the night and some cross-country was planned. It was April 2, but it was particularly cold this morning for this time of year. Cross-country would keep him warm from the outset, though.

With a large glass of water and a small orange juice, he was ready to take on the first task of the day: seven miles around the lanes and fields of north Lincoln. But first, he needed to select the mood music: Rap, House, or Garage for fast, short-burst workouts, for the beat, not the words; Pink Floyd or Fleetwood Mac for the long, slow, contemplative runs; and opera when slightly depressed or running off an injury or hangover. Today, it was the Fun Lovin' Criminals, music to really run to – so full steam ahead, then.

The morning air was fresh, chilly even, so Chris donned a bright yellow woollen running hat and running gloves. The hat was to protect his slightly male-pattern balding head, not that he really needed it; it was just a precaution, you understand! It also hid his now almost white crew-cut hair. The gloves were because he hated having cold hands. The prickly heat and chilblains were mementoes from a long-forgotten past.

He was quickly off down Castle Hill Lane, turning left and along Burton Road, with its array of local convenience shops and boutiques, even an award-winning chippy, but none of them open yet, of course. He was heading out into the countryside, using one of the more direct routes, quickly getting to the country road along Burton Road cliff top, which gave him an 'as far as the eye could see' panoramic vista of Lincolnshire's beautiful rolling countryside, normally full of sheep, Lincoln Red beef cattle, or arable farms. Often, while out on this regular route, a highlight was seeing red kites, or maybe a peregrine falcon or two looking for mice or voles.

The views went on for miles and miles; the vista never failed to take his breath away. Within ten minutes, he had found his stride. His pace for his age was surprisingly quick, with a strong gait.

He treated running like a type of therapy, allowing each footfall to banish even the darkest, most morose memories to the outer reaches of his normally calm mind. Today was no exception. As with many of his morning runs over the last few difficult months, the trials and tribulations of life started to seem small and once again surmountable, giving him, along with a small adrenaline hit, renewed optimism.

The weather felt perfect for running, chilly but not too cold, although not the winter cold which punched you in the throat with every breath, reduced your lung capacity by half, and made your legs feel like lead weights had been attached while you weren't looking.

It was just starting to get light and the dawn chorus was in full swing, not that he could hear it. Without too much effort, he was deep in the Lincolnshire countryside, admiring the views and thinking of nothing in particular. Calmness wrapped around him like Tilly's bright orange comfort blanket. Amusingly, it was a permanent fixture, being taken absolutely everywhere, every day, no matter what, no matter where. A team of explosive experts could not have prised it out of her small, tight, perfectly formed fist. Finally, the threadbare sliver of the blanket had been replaced with her first soft toy – a giraffe bought from Twycross Zoo. Next, a meerkat from the same place; a year later, with a massive change in direction, a Pony Royale, which was actually a unicorn. Currently, it was a real-life African grey parrot called Mr Nips which now occupied much of Tilly's time at home, and despite many practical objections by Sophie, he had become an extended member of the Beem family.

These were the inane, endorphin-induced thoughts which rattled around in Chris' near-empty head.

He stopped for a drink of Powerade about forty minutes into the run when he spotted something curious. Despite the hundreds of times he had completed this circuit, he had never noticed the ancient, almost primaeval red Massey Ferguson tractor, which was completely welded into the deep, brown, almost black mud of the field due to the twenty or more years of sitting idly in the same spot. Its rusted carcass looked like it was growing out of the earth, rather than slipping gracefully into the field.

He soon realised the hedge had just received its early spring haircut. The farmer seemed to have been a bit brutal, probably hoping it would last all year, and this had exposed the tractor to road users for the first time in donkey's years.

Chris held on to a handful of fond family memories, which only really extended to his grandfather who had been an arable farmer from the late 40s onwards. He had owned a near-identical tractor. In a snap decision, he decided to take a closer, albeit a quick look, before he started to get cold and stiff.

As he approached, he started to think maybe it was not worth the effort. The tractor was no more than a shell of muddy parts, a skeleton of its former self; just birds' nests, rust, and memories. Then, just as he had decided to continue his run, he caught sight of something blue with a yellow frame with a small flashing light, the type cyclists used on the front of their bikes. He realised it was this slow flashing light which had caught his eye, thus drawing him towards the old tractor. It was something which had no place being there, so now he felt compelled to investigate further. As he got closer, he realised the blue and yellow block was a rucksack of some description. He could not quite see the dimensions, but he was sure that was what it was. He had plenty of his own to be able to identify that it was not only a rucksack but a new one. Curiosity drove him to take the few extra steps which were needed to finally pull alongside the tractor. Now within arm's reach of the bag, he, without knowing why, gave a furtive little look around, to see if he was being watched. He couldn't immediately see anyone or anything to give him that impression, but for some reason, his heckles were up, along with his blood pressure and his heart rate.

He reached out and made a grab for it. Just as he did so, a large coal-black rook squawked loudly, then screeched away from behind the rear wheel. He practically jumped out of his skin and, in the process, he slipped on the wet grass, landing hard next to the front wheel. This had the effect of shaking free the rucksack, which then seemed to slowly release its grip on the wing mirror. Now free from being intertwined with the rusted, web-filled, and mirrorless wing mirror, it landed square in the middle of Ron Hill's finest tracksters and simply sat there, waiting patiently for Chris to make the next move.

His heart pounded wildly in his chest, making him feel out of breath. Despite the running to get to this point, it was a strange sensation. Then, for some unexplainable reason, he once again looked about him. It was like he knew he was doing something wrong, but what was he doing wrong, he didn't know. First left, then right, then a full 360 degrees. Confident he was alone – after all, it was still early in the morning – he slowly and cautiously unzipped the top external opening of the rucksack, then took another quick furtive look around before peeking inside. The zip, being new, was stiff and became stuck while it was only partially opened. He could just see through the tiny gap, just enough to make his heart race even more and just enough to make him race home. He carried the rucksack on his back, as they were designed to be used, thus raising no suspicious looks along the way. He definitely did not want to get stopped with this content.

Chapter Three

Once home, Chris headed straight into his office and for the first time in twenty-three years, he locked the door. He dropped the rucksack on the floor and slumped into his chair, absolutely exhausted, partly because the rucksack was heavy – it must have weighed fifty-five pounds at least – and partly because he had virtually sprinted the three miles home, all the time making sure no one saw him or had time to register anything about him. These precautions surprised him, on reflection. After all, he hadn't done anything wrong – yet. This had made the run home something of a nightmare, as he altered his route, doubled back, and eventually took the longest way possible, including scaling a small fence to avoid the main track into his lane. All this left him tired, wet, a little scared and very much on edge.

He sat motionless, listening to his heartbeat slowly returning to its normal resting rhythm, the cold sweat drying with a few prickly reminders that he had been running just as fast as he could. Once his pulse and breathing were somewhere near normal, he started to relax a little when suddenly, the handle of his office door rattled roughly and a muffled, "What on earth!" came from the other side. "What's going on?" Rattle. *"Are you okay?"* Rattle, rattle. "Is everything all right? Can you let me in, please?" All this in just four seconds of desperate rattle-kick-rattle pleading.

Reacting quickly, he kicked the rucksack hard, hurting his big toe in the process, and lodging it among the several others he had in his ever-growing collection of nearly 'out of action' kits. His you-never-know-when-it-may-come-in-handy attitude was, for once, coming in useful at this moment.

He unlocked and opened the door as quickly as possible, with his brain spinning while it searched for a plausible excuse. He was face to face with Tilly, who simply said, "Oh! Hi, Dad. Have you seen Mr Nips? He's missing, and you know how much Mum wants an excuse to get rid of him."

Chris nearly passed out there and then. The relief of not having to lie, especially to Tilly, was palpable.

Tilly stood looking at Chris with an amused expression on her face. It was like she could read the lie which had just been wiped from his mind. She had always had the measure of her dad and instinctively knew his mood, even when he didn't.

"What have you been up to?" she enquired with a half-smile forming on her lips. "Have you won the lottery?" she teased, reaching down to retrieve a crisp new £20 note from beside his right foot. Chris was just about to make up something about finding it while out running – he had found quite a lot of odds and sods over the years – but never a new £20 note. A scabby old fiver, maybe!

Just then, a loud crash and a familiar shrill squawk sounded from the kitchen, spurring Matilda into immediate action. Saving his blushes, she rushed off, still clutching the £20, to salvage the situation and to clean up any mess prior to the arrival of Mum, who was just finishing up in the bathroom.

Chris cursed himself under his breath. Kicking the rucksack must have released a lone prisoner from its contents. Now Tilly had it for her school fees – today's day trip to The Deep in Hull, one of the seemingly daily extracurricular activities which attracted extra fees at an already expensive private school.

He made sure everything looked its usual mess, then went about his normal routine, ditching the trainers and kit by the door, dashing upstairs for a quick shower, and changing into black 501 jeans and a suitably sports logoed T-shirt, ready to face the working day. Today, he was more mindful of how quickly events could change, if the rucksack had anything to do with it.

He sat sipping strong black coffee at the kitchen table with Tilly and Sophie, continually refusing the usual offers of toast or cereal. He was not one for breaking fast before noon, not out of any conviction, but breakfast always gave him chronic indigestion.

Sophie asked Chris about his plans for the day, enquiring what they might have for dinner that evening. He offered to cook his signature Chilli con Carne as both his girls loved that. It was the food equivalent of an apology to Sophie, who seemed to silently accept, reaching out and gently placing her hand on his arm. Once again, he felt all was well in the world.

The girls started discussing and deciding what was needed for their own day's activities, and fetched from different rooms or retrieved from under beds the necessary items. Then they were once again ready to set off for work and school.

Tilly was always ready on time and keen to get to the Lincoln Minster. The original school had been established nearly two hundred years ago as an independent co-ed preparatory and senior school. It had been moved to its current premises in 1996, and with nice symmetry, the building was the exact same age as the founding of the schools. Being within easy walking distance of home was an added bonus, but that wasn't the reason the school had been chosen for her.

It was because it was one of the best in the country for exam results and overall pupil achievement. Some of the brightest minds had attended this seat of learning, including Alfred, Lord

Tennyson, and Lady Thatcher. Tennyson attended King Edward VI Grammar School; Margaret Thatcher attended Kesteven and Grantham, just some of the schools which were amalgamated to form Lincoln Minster. Chris still admired Thatcher for her deft handling during a sovereign invasion and a national power crisis, both these conflicts happening simultaneously in 1982. Additionally, Tilly had a supportive group of bright, inquisitive, and bubbly friends there.

Sophie, however, had an all-consuming, distressing job working at the job centre. She was always exhausted at the end of the day with tales which made him blanch.

He acknowledged the anger, depression, and sheer hopelessness of Lincolnshire's thirteen thousand or so unemployed, all desperate for a fresh start and finding it practically impossible to make one. He was beginning to know just how they felt.

Chris, on the other hand, had a job he loved and was good at, using the creative side of his Piscean brain and feeding his unflinching obsession with all things technical. Like most people who could master the vagaries of information technology and the complex but often baffling internet, he found it mentally and physically liberating. This vocation allowed him the enviable opportunity to work from home. There, he created bespoke multimedia, and highly interactive, innovative, and cutting-edge websites.

Recently, in fact, over the last twelve months, his thriving little business had taken a turn for the worse, beyond the usual market downturn and localised recession. It was something else. He couldn't put his finger on it, but this was clearly and evidently the root of the mounting tensions between him and Sophie. As hard as he tried to shield her from it, money did make the world go around. Well, a certain amount of it, anyway, and not having any of it was not an option. These were his pressing worries.

He continued to sit at the breakfast table for a few more minutes, thinking through the recent challenges. Everything always seemed to start well, with the usual initial meetings with clients to agree on the scope and rough design of the website. Work could then continue in his multi-purpose office. Normally, the clients gave him the freedom to control all aspects of the work and he had hit every deadline, so why had it all changed?

In the last six months, his once-thriving business had taken a dramatic downward spiral. His normally loyal and lucrative clients had been eloping to India where a web designer could cost as little as a Starbucks coffee, instead of the salary of a Starbucks coffee house manager. This, coupled with the worst credit crunch he could recall, had made many doom-mongers begin to draw similarities with the 1980s recession. Then, the whole country had nearly buckled under the strain of mass unemployment, sky-high inflation, and an intense class war. This was before a real war happened which would galvanise the country. Right now, though, things were not good, not good at all.

He believed the whole mess would become a self-fulfilling prophecy if the media didn't let up a bit. *It's the recession* that had become the mantra of once happy clients. What really hurt him was clients agreeing to the work, him getting started, and then at the last minute, and often after Chris had invested time and money in the project, they would, out of the blue, cancel. No redress, no money back, no client.

He had decided to challenge one potential client who had pulled the plug at the last minute, but all he got for his trouble was a curt e-mail saying they didn't want any trouble and didn't know what he was mixed up in, it wasn't their concern, and not to call again. He was shocked but had hit a dead end. Maybe his desperation for work had started to show and was putting off new clients. Even more surprisingly, it was also putting off existing clients who would normally allow him to maintain their web pages, but that also was becoming a thing of the past.

He had, despite his best efforts with improved quality, lost eighty-five per cent of his client base. Boy, was it starting to show – red letters, red bills, and red eyes from the stresses and strains. He believed he now knew how Sophie's clients felt, but he didn't burden her with all the facts. She had enough of that every minute of every working day. However, she knew the situation was becoming untenable, hence, the now frequent protracted and intense arguments which were always about money, the root of all evil. What would they do if he, as the main breadwinner, was not able to win bread? The nightmare they would enter if that came true was unimaginable. Everything was on the line, so he reassured her repeatedly that he would do whatever it took to safeguard everything. After all, they had both sacrificed so much to make a comfortable and secure life for them all, but especially for Tilly.

The invisible, microscopically slender thread of life's rich tapestry was there dangling. It was now being pulled by some unseen forces and their happy, content life was beginning to unravel at such a rate of knots, that he wasn't sure he really could pull a rabbit out of the hat. He was running out of tricks, running out of ideas, and running out of time.

He continued to struggle daily, though, determined to weather the storm. That was until he had stumbled upon the rotting Massey Ferguson, with its innocent-looking rucksack.

He shook himself out of his self-induced trance, immediately stopped what he was doing, went back into his office, and for only the second time in twenty-three years, he locked the door.

Chapter Four

Chris gingerly pulled out the rucksack from his own pile of stuff and took a long hard look at it. It was, in fact, a blue Puma rucksack with very distinctive light blue stripes and a yellow handle with its own built-in warning light which Chris had switched off earlier. There was also a small sun in the middle of a white circle that had been stitched onto the middle of the outer panel which made it look like a smiley face, not a design Chris had seen before, more flag than a logo, but it could be some football team colours and club logo, for all he knew. He did know the bag had a 30 litre capacity; it said so on a plastic label dangling from the top flap, the one you normally pulled off upon purchase. It also confirmed it was constructed of a totally waterproof Gore-Tex, which would keep the contents completely dry in all weathers, except underwater, he thought. Its top flap was held in place by quick-release clips, the shoulder straps and sternum strap were easily adjustable, and there was a zip pocket on the rear along with a zipped main compartment. One final detail was the yellow loop used to hang it on changing room hooks. He carefully popped the clips, and with significant effort, unzipped the stiff external zipper and looked inside. There were about five new £20 notes poking out through the secure zip of the main compartment and a couple just sitting there, teasing him, giving the appearance of having been zipped up in a hurry and a few notes had come free and gone unnoticed. This told him two things: one, it certainly contained – maybe real, maybe fake –

British pounds; two, he was the first person to look inside since it was zipped shut.

So how much could the main compartment hold if it were full? It was large enough to hold a life-changing amount of money. The prospect was very compelling.

The main zipped compartment was secured by an overly large, new-looking combination lock which did not budge when he tried to manually prise it open. No matter how much he pulled or twisted, it stubbornly refused to allow access.

He sipped his now cold espresso and considered his options: slice it open across the base, or force open the zip on either side of the central lock. But, not knowing the exact contents, or to whom it belonged, he would be committing a criminal act, at the very least criminal damage. It was possible that it could have been discarded by an organised crime gang, even an unorganised one. That would constitute receiving stolen goods or proceeds of crime – jail time for sure. Or, unlikely as it seemed, but still a real possibility, a terrorist group. Boy, he was really reaching now, but instantly the 7/7 London bombings sprang to mind. He had been on holiday at the time but had been using the Circle Line tube weekly back then to see a client at Aldgate. It had really shaken him up at the time. This could turn out to be dangerous or it could even be booby-trapped.

Bloody hell, BOOBY trapped! Where did that come from? Was he really so spooked by this innocent-looking rucksack, despite its not-so-innocent contents?

He hadn't thought about that when he had strapped on the rucksack and ran home. It had certainly felt heavy enough to contain absolutely anything, and now he really started to think about it, yes, even explosives! Only now did the alarm bells really start ringing. "A bit late though, don't you think?" he silently whispered to himself.

He cursed, this time aloud, at his own lack of imagination.

Especially with his first-hand knowledge of the devastation explosives could have in the wrong hands, or even more so in the right hands, as proven by the IRA litter bin bombs. He had seen many such devices in Northern Ireland in the early eighties, while on foot patrol with Lima Company, 42 Commando. He knew he would never forget the aftermath of one of the most destructive ways to say 'fuck you' imaginable, for as long as he lived. Some things remained, always there in the subconscious. It didn't matter that you hadn't given them a second thought for ten, fifteen, or even twenty years, they never disappeared completely. Sporty types call it muscle memory; Chris called it experience.

So, if this were a sincere consideration, he should have thought about it whilst sitting beside the tractor. But why the hell would he? It wasn't Northern Ireland during the troubles. They were long since passed and an uneasy peace now reigned throughout. Back then, he would have known better, that's for sure. But now! No.

He started to calm down a little and felt it may well be subliminal messages creeping into his mind. The news was crammed full of horrific details from the never-ending fatal attacks using Improvised Explosive Devices known as IEDs, which were killing and maiming our young British soldiers weekly, nearly daily. Reports from Afghanistan or Iraq by some gung-ho journalist trying to make a name – fear sells, mortality sells more. As a former captain in the Marines, he felt the underlying pain associated with these stories more than most. He glanced at his wall-mounted service medals, and with a nod to his past, he decided from now on he would apply a little of some of his hard-earned experience through his specialist training. So, with the adrenalin levels turned up to maximum, now applying a higher level of caution which maybe had been understandably somewhat lacking, he thought he knew how to proceed.

As he unhurriedly began, he remembered a story he had often told others which was orated to him by an old friend, Karl (Pinkie) Pinkstone, a major in the Royal Engineers. He had told him the story during a drunken officers' mess Christmas ball, in all its gory graphic detail, putting him right off his Eton mess in the process. Pinkie had, at one time, during a house clearance in Aden in 1975, come across just about every conceivable type of booby trap. Apparently, what the Somali people lacked in firearms, they more than made up for in improvisation. Right down to a small explosive device under the fresh bottle of milk in a fridge in a recently cleared combatants dwelling which, upon removal, broke a small circuit and created an electrical arc. In turn, it had ignited the 3 oz of Semtex and completely ripped the hand and most of the arm off the thirsty, thieving squaddie. He had also gone on to describe how everyday objects are easily booby-trapped by using common, easily obtained items like fishing line to create a type of ripcord which would trigger an explosion, but only when manually activated, meaning they could remain active for years. It was called being wired for sound; the sound was pain and screaming, mostly.

It was surprising what you remembered when your senses were heightened, which Chris' now definitely were because he knew, I mean really knew, this was wrong, all over wrong.

Now, bearing all this in mind, he started to apply the modicum of common sense he had been missing so far. First, he looked over the rucksack from top to bottom, but there were no obvious outward signs of interference, tampering, or booby-trapping. Had he really expected any? Would there be some exposed wires or tell-tale clues, like you see in the movies? Well, of course, there weren't. Next, frustrated and running out of options, he examined the lock – no wires, free from any corrosion or scratches. In fact, it looked brand-new.

He twiddled the combination randomly at first, but on getting no joy there, he started to go through the series of numbers, just like anyone would – 111, 222, 333, etc. This went on for nearly an hour. Feeling the natural frustration of failure, he had an unhealthy desire to just rip it apart, but he could not bring himself to do it. Then he thought he would try a number he regularly used. It was the same number, easy to remember, that he used for the combination of his bike lock, the home alarm, and even the shed. Lazy, yes, but it also had meaning to him. In a last-ditch attempt, he slowly, making sure he got the numbers in the correct alignment, tried 3... 8... 1... It was easy to remember because it meant three words, eight letters, one meaning; simply *I Love You*. It was the code he had used to sign off his e-mails to Sophie while they were first courting, you know, before it was officially the *I love you* moment. He still used it today when he sent an e-mail to her work, not wanting to potentially embarrass her in front of her work colleagues, as they shared terminals.

To his surprise and concern, the lock snapped open at the last alignment of the 1. Could this really be a coincidence?

No, it could not. He already knew, of course not.

He felt compelled to continue, having already gone this far. Slowly, he began to unzip the main compartment. His hands were shaking and sweat was starting to appear on his brow and upper lip. He continued at a glacial pace, checking for electrical wires, fishing lines, and any outward signs of tampering. Nothing. Nearly there, he gently opened the main, now fully unzipped compartment, and started to look inside. At that exact moment, his mobile rang loudly. Startled, he dropped the rucksack and the contents – mostly an avalanche of money – fluttered and clattered over the floor of his office.

Chapter Five

The mobile call had been from a nice young lady, telling him he had recently had an accident. He must have totally forgotten about it, but she nevertheless reassured him he could claim compensation. When she asked him when he had had the accident, Chris told her it would be tomorrow morning at 11 a.m., which would probably be the most convenient time for any accident. She had, for some strange reason, abruptly hung up. Rude.

Chris sat staring at the contents of the rucksack strewn across his office floor, feeling a wave of emotions. Firstly shock – well, the contents would surprise anyone – then fear. Fear of what was coming. These contents were a harbinger of doom for sure.

It wasn't a long interruption, but he had been so absorbed with his office floor, that he hadn't realised it was nearly 1 p.m. and he hadn't even started the storyboarding for the layout of the Lincoln City Football Club's new website. The Managing Director wanted it to be user-friendly, whilst at the same time drawing in as much money from the supporters as possible. In other words, make it sticky, meaning keep visitors on the site, if possible, without them feeling fleeced. Being one of only two clients this year, it meant he could not afford to lose this special opportunity, so he really had to shift his attention away from the contents of the rucksack and back to the job at hand.

However, he could not just leave it lying there – the possibilities were just too intriguing. Surely even this special one had to wait, he reasoned. At the very least, he had to pick up its contents which had spewed all over his office floor. If someone had lost it and not left it, they were already £20 down thanks to Tilly!

He was stunned by what the rucksack contained. A handgun with a detachable silencer fitted a stack of black and white A5 photographs held together with a large silver bulldog clip, an A4 manila envelope with 'Christopher Beem' written on it in tidy blue copperplate handwriting, and more money than he had ever seen in one place at one time in his entire life.

Chris picked up the pistol and examined it with the expertise of a man who was used to handling firearms. He knew from experience it was genuine; it was also clean and well-oiled. The smell of gun oil was something he had once been extremely familiar with. It housed what looked like a full magazine of live rounds. Blank rounds had distinctive crimping, but these contained lead encased in copper, just like the real thing.

He placed it in the top drawer of his desk, the only one which locked properly, then locked it.

He then quickly picked up the money strewn all over the floor. It felt real, it looked real, only time would tell. He stacked it into an A3 cardboard file tidy, roughly counting as he did so. There were approximately £350,000 in £20s as £5,000 bundles, secured with those red bank bands, no name. Plus £160 loose, minus the £20. And just for good measure, there was a box of 9 mm ammunition, certainly real, to go along with the pistol, buried amongst all that cash.

The ammo also went in the locked drawer.

The file tidy, now crammed with money and the lid firmly taped on, was placed under his desk.

He quickly flicked through the photos as some had come

away from the clip – all individuals, taken apparently without their knowledge, not posed. Five men and one woman, the pictures taken at various times and in different locations, some even at night. Nothing immediately jumped out at him. His first impression was that they looked like early recce shots.

For a man who had not thought about his service days for two decades or more, he was spending a lot of time thinking about it now.

He nervously opened the manila envelope with his name on it, knowing this would reveal the true nature of the contents. He knew it would require immediate action – nobody went to all this trouble just to make your day. It contained two folded sheets of A4 lined paper.

Entitled 'YOUR KILL LIST', in neat blue handwriting, he was left in no doubt what this list represented, but why? It was a list of six full names, including the sort of titles that signified profession, official position, and gender.

No one on the list was known to him personally or professionally, as far he could see, so no clear meaning could be inferred from the list alone, even if its title had left nothing to the imagination. A lot of research would be needed to understand what the list really meant.

He straightened up his office, putting it back to its scruffy best, apart from the hidden cash, the hidden gun, and a brand-new target list, that is. He just had enough time before he had to crack on with the LCFC storyboard to run a quick Google search. He was, after all, an accomplished silver surfer.

Very soon, the contents of his good luck find would get his undivided attention.

As a matter of life or death.

Chapter Six

He was still doing his first rapid research scan of the list, using the Apple Mac at the kitchen table, when Tilly dashed in from school. She had some research of her own to do and seeing Dad using the Mac, she naturally assumed it would be okay to use his office computer. After all, the research for her history homework would only take thirty minutes or so, especially with the new faster 128-bit broadband, which had been a vital business if costly, upgraded only last month. The blur of movement caught his attention, and seeing her heading to his office, he jumped to his feet, dashing like a racing whippet across the room, intent on getting ahead of Tilly.

He need not have worried, however. He had untidied up well, leaving nothing incriminating in view. He wasn't used to all this deceit. It had him on edge. Their family life had been so normal, so peaceful, so open and transparent, until this morning's run.

He was reverting to type, something he did not want to happen at any cost, not after the massive effort it had taken, over many years, to make it all go away. He had reinvented himself once, but never again.

It wouldn't have mattered anyway. Tilly had gone directly upstairs to change out of her distinctive blue and green Minster uniform which she adored so much, right down to the compulsory Dickensian school cap.

Although he had put things away, he had overlooked the

43

rucksack, which he now quickly stuffed once again amongst his group of battered, bruised, and mud-strewn old rucksacks. However, it looked oddly out of place, being so new and clean, like a diamond on a pile of dung.

He decided to risk leaving it for now but would move it tomorrow to a more secure location.

Chris had decided he wouldn't broach the subject of the rucksack with Sophie tonight. Last night's argument was still too raw and fresh, and he didn't want to risk opening that particular wound again so soon. He wasn't in any great rush to decide what to do with the contents. Despite his obvious need for money, he just didn't know what the real cost would be, and after all, it wasn't really his. He would need to sleep on it but right now, he had a job to do.

Tilly came skipping in, which was no mean feat as she also had Mr Nips perched on her shoulder. She placed him carefully on the arm of the battered office chair. They chatted for a little while, then she went about completing her homework, using the internet for her research. History at her fingertips – had being a school kid ever been easier? I think not.

She had her own log-in, although access to the darker, sleazier recesses of Pandora's worldwide pleasure box was severely restricted. Chris, ever parentally vigilant, plus being fully aware of the harm, both mental and possibly physical, had applied some high-level restrictions. Tilly called them the parental controls from hell, despite the fact he had set them up for her safety. There were some strange people with some strange practices and he didn't want her to be vulnerable for even a nanosecond.

He knew the dangers of the internet and social networking sites. He had a friend in the police cyber-crimes unit who had, in no uncertain terms, told him to restrict access, and why. The why had shocked him so badly that he had, for the time being, blocked all but Bebo (lame-o Bebo, according to Tilly). He insisted that this had to be paid for by him, as an extra precaution. This gave him dual access, allowing him to monitor the content if he ever thought it was necessary. Tilly was actually just as savvy as any tech specialist, with the maturity of a thirty-five year old, and sometimes the attitude to go with it. He had also taken the ability to remove the search history or archive the cookies list out of Tilly's hands, so he could always see exactly what she had been viewing. Tilly knew this, so it made for open and honest use of the internet. Nothing was more important than the safety of his family. It was a cliché, he knew that, but deep in his heart, he also knew he meant it right down through his whole core, his whole being and, if possible, beyond.

Chris patiently waited for Sophie to get home from work so he could attend his LCFC appointment, which was right across town in an area known as Sincil Bank and would require at least thirty-five minutes during rush hour.

Sophie arrived later than expected, which left no real opportunity for greetings, just a *hello, goodbye, Tilly is in the office doing her homework, must dash, see you later*, type of exchange.

The traffic was worse than he had recently experienced, always the same when you don't leave yourself a little buffer zone of time. He was just five minutes late, so not a disaster. *Have you seen the traffic?* would normally suffice.

However, Phil Dorian's PA told Chris that he had just left very abruptly with an elegant lady, in a large Mercedes-Benz limousine, with unusual private plates. Phil hadn't told her why. He had, however, told her he did not want to rearrange the meeting with Beem.

Chris sat fuming in his car, unable to move, afraid his temper would cause him to crash if he set off before he could calm himself down. Now had he lost another client, this time through his own stupidity. His mantra had always been 'five minutes early is ten minutes late'. He prided himself on his timekeeping, a throwback from his service days. It was as important today as it had always been to him. He had let himself down and worst of all, he had let Sophie and Tilly down.

Why hadn't he just finished the brief this morning, as planned? He could have dropped it off and conducted the meeting via phone, meaning he wouldn't have been caught out by Sophie's late arrival, the appalling traffic down Lincoln's three-mile-long high street, or the mysterious visitor.

Still, he wondered, who was the woman who had whisked Phil away so abruptly, and why no further contact? Afraid of making things worse, he decided he had to leave it for a while and do his best to secure another client.

Dinner was a quiet affair that night. Chris was brooding over the loss of LCFC and Sophie was upset, blaming herself, despite Chris reassuring her that it was him who had let the day slip away. It was all his fault. He decided this was not the time to mention the real distraction, which could turn out to be his financial saviour or his doom. Either way, it would look different in the morning. He hoped.

On top of everything else, Tilly was mad at him because the computer and evidently the laptop had blocked her from all the 'mega-cool' sites.

They always tried to eat at the table as a family, to catch up on the day. Well, not today. No one wanted to relive this day, so dinner was over very quickly and quietly, along with the rest of the evening.

In bed, while Sophie purred like a pedigree cat, he stared at the ceiling and reflected on the day. For a woman who thrashed about like a whirling dervish, she always seemed to sleep so soundly. What a day! Sleep was going to be hard to come by, the contents of the rucksack had made sure of that. So many options played across his mind, like the prizes on the conveyer belt of the Generation Game. What did it all mean? What was he going to do with the bloody list? Was he really tempted to risk everything for the money?

Chapter Seven

Beem started off the day as normal – run, shower, and coffee – as did the girls – shower, breakfast, dash off to school, and work.

He then went into his office and for only the third time, locked the door. But this time, he was determined it would be the last. Today he would either get rid of the rucksack or deposit it, along with its contents, in a better, more secure location. He didn't expect to keep them very long, but every minute was a risk.

For now, he lined the contents up in front of him, ready for a more detailed inspection. There was the large pile of money, the handgun with its detachable silencer, and the list along with the photos, which he now assumed were to be used collectively.

He sat there and just stared at the contents for a good twenty minutes, his mind spinning with possibilities – how, what, why, where, and wow, definitely wow. He took a deep breath and decided to start with the money. On examination, the money looked real – you know, used, non-sequential notes, and all that. It was stacked in bundles of £20 notes. He started to count. Finally, two hours and forty-five minutes, two recounts and three espressos later, the grand – and I do mean grand – total was £374,980, in non-sequential sterling notes. As far as he could tell, the notes were unmarked, there were no ink dyes, no magnesium powder, no metal strips which could act like transponders and no GPS locators. He had watched a lot of CSI: NY on TV so naturally he 'knew' all there was to know about this kind of cash drop. Usually, it was a ransom. What he needed to ascertain was when he was going to be held to ransom and for what.

He had never seen or even imagined this amount of cash before, and never thought he would, especially in this current cash-strapped climate. His brain wandered around and kept landing on just two of the endless possibilities: the money could be put towards Tilly's school fees, which were due in a month, and the annual mortgage payment, also due in a few months. Eventually, he pumped the brakes. He had to see the bigger picture. £374,980 in mostly used bills! He had read enough crime novels to know there was always a catch, but what the catch was, he couldn't be sure, yet! He was starting to see he was the catch, someone's catch of the day! This money was the bait. He couldn't help flicking through the bundles. Were they forgeries? Possibly. Could he keep the money? Possibly. Was it worth breaking his own moral guidelines for? Would he abandon all common laws of the land? Definitely not. So, what to do next?

He needed time to think this through. There was no immediate rush, he could sit on the money for a while, figure it all out. Surely that would do no harm. Additionally, he would also need to discuss and agree on a plan of action with Sophie – a decision which could make or break their family was not one he could or would take in isolation. Sophie had always kept him grounded, but only to the degree that Chris let her in. She acted as the voice of reason, even when he had his Black Dog days. In today's terms, it would be called PTSD. She had been there to console, rationalise and soothe. She didn't know half of it really, or she may not have been so rational, so calm.

What would he discuss with Sophie? Yes, the contents, but what was there to really discuss? He didn't yet know what any of it meant, and that would surely be her very first question.

He decided the best next action was to see if the handgun

was capable of firing, just in case. He wasn't going to use it, was he? It certainly looked real. He didn't immediately recognise the make or model, but a quick look on the net told him it was a Bersa Thunder 380 pistol fitted with a custom-made silencer – an Argentinian service issue weapon. He didn't suppose South America had very tight gun control laws, so it was probably relatively cheap and easy to purchase. Still, it was an unusual choice. On further inspection, he found it to have a bottom-mounted 9 mm calibre, 15-round capacity magazine, and rear cocking mechanism with a 90 degree safety clip. With a red dot showing up, the gun was safe and wouldn't shoot. He couldn't see a serial number on it anywhere; he had to assume it had been removed to stop it from having a firing history. It looked used, but it was clean and well-oiled. There were twenty-seven rounds in an ammunition box, a spare magazine. Oh boy, this brought back long-buried, dark, best-forgotten, memories. He felt the weightiness of the pistol in his right hand; it was a familiar, even comfortable, feeling. He knew a pistol like this could be used as protection, as persuasion, to threaten, as a deterrent, or something altogether more sinister. It could also be used to kill – after all, that was its main purpose – but what would its relationship be to him?

He hated to admit it even to himself, but it felt good to be holding a weapon again after all these years. It made him feel invincible again. He felt he now knew it would turn out to be sinister – guns don't just turn up so you could feel like James Bond, even for a little while.

He had no idea how correct this feeling was going to be.

Chapter Eight

He decided that first, he would hide the money and the gun away from prying eyes and curious little fingers just in case, before he considered what to do with the content of the manila envelope and photos. He thoroughly recleaned the gun, then wrapped it in a dry tea towel and placed it in a zip-lock plastic bag; training had taught him to respect firearms, especially if you intended to use them or maybe to dispose of them without fingerprints plastered all over. Then he carefully placed it, with all the money, into one of his tatty, but essentially waterproof rucksacks. This particular one he had even used in the Marines – it should have been thrown out long, long ago, but some bizarre desire to preserve memories had always stopped him.

Once it was all secure, he pulled the rucksack onto his shoulder, unlocked the office door and headed outside. He wanted to hide this poison chalice of booty in a more secure and hopefully secret place, away from prying eyes, especially Sophie and, of course, the mini super sleuth called Tilly.

Tilly seemed to have some kind of built-in radar for things you're not supposed to touch, and a habit of finding anything which was not meant to be found. Like the time she found Christmas presents, which had been stored in a heavy wardrobe, four days prior to the 25th. A three-year-old Tilly had squeezed her little frame through the tiniest gap in the wardrobe door. Sophie and Chris, having not heard a peep out of her for several hours, had gone searching for her, in a bit of a panic. When they eventually found her, she had opened them all and responded to their shock with, 'never mind, Dad. Father Christmas will bring me some more,' and of course, he had. He let these happy memories float around for a few more seconds, and then headed for the door. Just as he reached for the handle, there was a thunderously loud knock on the door.

Chris jumped out of his skin, pulling his hand away like the door handle was red hot. Bang! Another loud rap, like a man was using a sledgehammer as a knocker. Once he had jumped back into his skin, he threw the rucksack across the room where it came to rest under the dining room table, then more slowly than he had intended, he opened the door. He was slightly shocked to find, standing on the other side, the postman.

Shocked because this was an abnormally large postman who had granite-looking hands the size of snow shovels, and boulders for shoulders which a Mr Universe, World's Strongest Man contestant, or even a World Wrestling Federation (WWF) wrestler would have been proud of.

Clearly, this was not his usual postman; his regular postman had the total body mass of just one of this guy's arms.

WWF delivered a small plain brown parcel. Chris thanked him for waiting, took the proffered parcel, signed the requested tracking slip, and he took one more look at the gargantuan bear of a man. The postman just gave a lazy half-smile then, without a word, he ambled slowly away, blocking out the sun as he went.

Rude!

He sat at the dining room table, inspected the exterior, and then opened the parcel. Inside was full of roughly torn-up newspapers as padding which surprisingly were dated today. At the bottom was a family photo – his family – taken last August whilst holidaying in Crete. On the back, written in elegant copperplate handwriting, it simply said:

I see you have got our package.

Chris felt a cold shiver dance down his spine. He knew this was about the rucksack, but what did it really mean?

He dashed out of the door, hoping to catch the postman who he thought might be able to provide some missing pieces of this increasingly confusing puzzle. On reflection, he did not look anything like a genuine postman. He was the size of a walking billboard, only he couldn't figure out what that message could be. You don't send a half man-mountain, half mountain gorilla unless it is a serious message.

WWF was nowhere to be seen; he must have been in a motor vehicle to disappear so completely, so quickly. He gave one more contemplative look and headed back indoors.

He sat back down at the dining room table, trying to think, trying to expand the limits of his imagination, not doing a particularly good job. He was being constrained by the normality of his life as it was these days. Suddenly, a key was in the lock and the door flew open with a bang as it slammed into the wall.

Tilly ran in, eyes everywhere, looking, searching. "Aha!" she said, "This will do." And she reached down under the table for his rucksack.

Chris reacted quickly and snatched it away just in time, abruptly shouting, "No! I need that! I'm heading for the gym!" Tilly jumped back, startled, unaccustomed to being spoken to in even the slightest of harsh tones, especially from Dad.

"I was only going to borrow it," she said. "We need a bag to carry our treasure. We are on a scavenger hunt with the school. My team's all outside waiting, now. I'm sorry," she finished, tears welling up in her eyes.

Chris dropped the rucksack behind him and pulled her close,

his heart pounding in his chest. "No! I'm sorry, Matilda. It's been one of those weeks. Please forgive me," was all he could say, his own voice quivering a little.

"Let me get you one of my old ones, then it won't matter if it gets even more damaged. Okay, beautiful?" He kissed the top of her head.

"Okay, Dad." She was smiling again, much to his relief.

He calmly went into the office, dragged another slightly less tatty rucksack off the shelf and gently gave it to Tilly. "Here, use this." He kissed her gently on the forehead, which had the effect of immediately erasing the incident from her mind, and with a spring in her step, off she raced, accidentally slamming the door again on the way out.

Chris sat there somewhere in the neighbourhood of shock and disgust at his own actions. What was going on with him? He had been so sure he would manage this. This was the second near-miss. He really must start acting like a grown-up and take care of the priorities, the first of which was to hide this lot, and quickly.

He scooped up the rucksack and headed for the door once again, this time mercifully without incident. Once outside, he headed across to the bottom left corner of the garden where, half-hidden by a huge weeping willow that he and Sophie had planted the year they had moved in, there was a shed – one he had built for himself. In the process, he had made sure it contained some pretty mod cons, including electricity, thermal heating, a large colour TV, a comfy chair, a small writing desk with an office chair, a laptop, an old Xbox, but best of all, a well-hidden secret safe. This was a place he had once envisioned would be a much-needed man cave to escape a large noisy child-infested house. Well, it hadn't turned out quite like that, but he still liked having his own space.

The safe looked for all the world exactly like the rest of the wooden floor panels, except these ones had the ability to lower slightly once pressure was applied in the correct spot. The panel then slid to the left, revealing a 3ft by 3ft mechanical combination locking safe – you could probably guess the combination – which was buried deep into the concrete base of the shed.

He had built it because they had been burgled within the first few months of moving in, so along with the alarm and security lights came a hidden safe. It was a place for anything of value, although admittedly they didn't have much of value right now. Regardless of that, it was a secure private place which only he and Sophie knew about. She didn't even have the combination, although she could probably guess it. So no one knew about it. At least, that's what he thought.

He opened the safe and looked inside to check the contents: some gold jewellery, some mementoes from his service days, two of Sophie's old rings more sentimental than valuable, a pair of expensive but broken watches kept for the same reason (one which did work – it was his late grandfather's), some old share certificates, near worthless in the recession. But the most valuable of all to him was the selection of baby photos of Tilly. They were irreplaceable. Finally, he had secretly kept, against all the advice, three black and white polaroid baby scans – they could have been the rest of his family.

He placed the old rucksack in the safe, changed the combination and relocked it, replaced the wooden panels, and checked it was still undetectable. It was.

He decided to get rid of the new rucksack before it could incriminate him. He just needed to devote some time to properly understand what he was doing. Yes, the letter was not very subtle in its message: we know you have the rucksack, we know you know what it holds, and we know where you live.

That's what they knew. Now, what did he know?

Nothing.

He still had to spend some time researching the list before he could have a much-needed heart-to-heart with Sophie.

His postal visit had given him a new sense of urgency, so first, he placed the manila envelope in the lockable drawer in his office, then went off to dispose of the rucksack. He drove his Volvo V70 Estate to the refuse collection point on the very edge of the Lincolnshire/Nottinghamshire border. He didn't want to use the local one; he wanted this to be as far away as possible. He had completely rendered the rucksack useless by ripping out the bottom, cutting off the shoulder straps and breaking the zip mechanism. No one would be recycling this baby.

Job done.

He took a leisurely drive home via the back roads. Driving relaxed him, helping him to think more clearly. His only thoughts were firmly fixed on the hand-delivered parcel from WWF this morning. What disturbed him most was the implications of the writing on the back of his family photo. Someone had meant for him to find and take the rucksack. They knew where he lived, they knew what he looked like, they could even have his signature – he had signed for the package. His initial fears were growing. If experience had taught him anything, it was to listen to his inner voice. A conscience pricked may well be a life saver; that inner voice, that second sight, had saved his life more than once. He still couldn't make any sense of it, not one bit. Why was he the recipient of the money, gun and that bloody list? One thing was clear: this was defiantly aimed at him.

Chapter Nine

By the time he got home, it was dusk, so this left him only a little time for research before he would be expected to cook for his girls. He headed straight to his office, not locking the door.

He started a file, putting the list of names on the inside cover, and the photos in the clear sleeves after he had wiped them all clean of his fingerprints, just in case he had to dispose of everything quickly.

There were six A5 black and white portrait photos of six different people, five men and one younger-looking woman of around thirty-eight who was in school uniform. He immediately recognised the badge but not the woman. He would have to research her. Maybe Tilly would know her from school. He took hold of each picture in its individual plastic sleeve in turn. There was a policeman, uniformed, who held a rank yet to be determined. There was a clergyman in cassocks, wearing what he knew to be a mitre or C of E bishop's hat. He had been a long-term patron of the Wig & Mitre Inn, located on Steep Hill, part of uphill Lincoln's main street. No internet was needed for this, but he was still going to be busy later. Next, a man in a business-type suit and the only person of colour, wearing some kind of official regalia sash. Again, over to the net. The penultimate one was a chef in whites and a logo on his chest which was too blurred to indicate where he was working. Finally, one was a builder in a yellow safety hard hat with FossWay Commercial Construction written down the side. No need for the all-knowing net here. FossWay Commercial Construction was a very well-known local company that employed thousands across the county. It had been a prosperous Lincolnshire building firm for decades, even more so since the University of Lincoln was approved, and then built by them. It had gone from strength to strength, culminating in the development of the much-loved Brayford Pool and surrounding area. All this beauty had been created from just an old rundown railway yard full of 1920 waterfront warehouses, including an abattoir. It was now a thriving varsity area of culture, with all the big-name pubs, clubs and restaurants enjoying the marina with waterfront views with its abundant colony of beautiful white swans, to rival any metropolis.

Written on the back of each photo, again in neat blue copperplate handwriting, were their DOBs. The schoolgirl who was actually a teacher had 29/2/73, making her thirty-nine years old, or ten depending on your point of view about leap years. The policeman had 6/9/59, making him fifty-two. The clergyman had 4/5/41, making him seventy. The businessman had 9/10/50, making him sixty-one.

The builder had 11/6/68, making him forty-three.

Finally, the chef had 1/4/76, making him the youngest male at thirty-six. They did not, certainly at first glance, seem to have anything in common. Neither their occupations, gender, colour, nor their ages were even close.

He had hoped the 'Kill List' would hold the key to this ever-growing mystery, but it hadn't. It simply married names to the relevant photo so he could put a face to a name, as it were. It didn't tell him why these lucky six had been chosen, nor their connection to each other or himself.

When no hard facts are to be found, the vacuum of

knowledge lets your imagination expand to fill the gap. What could it mean – a large sum of much-needed money, a small easily concealed and easy-to-use gun with a silencer fitted, along with six innocent-enough-looking photographs? The words 'Your mission, should you choose to accept it' filled the void, but this was Lincoln, often described as quaint and unspoilt, not Lincoln, Nebraska. This just didn't happen here, whatever 'this' was.

Chris had cooked and they had eaten as a family, Sophie and Tilly their usual chatty selves. He tried to contribute but kept drifting off into a world of his own. Luckily, his mental absence seemed to go unnoticed. Now, the house sat in quiet serenity, being too worn out by the vagaries of the day's challenges. He decided to call it a day and sleep on it. Perhaps if he did some detailed research into the people in the photos in the morning, as his first rapid search hadn't been nearly as productive as he had expected, he would find some answers. About to head to bed, he was suddenly enveloped in silent, pitch-black, breath-taking darkness. He stood stock-still, hoping a fuse had tripped, or there was a fault in the system. There was always going to be some other rational reason for what had occurred, so why was he so scared? In his heart, though, he knew it was all connected to the photographs. He waited for a beat and tried to adjust his night vision, watching for someone out there in the night. Spooked, he took out his phone, switched on the light feature, and keeping it low, gingerly made his way slowly to the fuse box in the kitchen. Flipping open the door, he discovered that it had, indeed, tripped. He flipped it and was immediately bathed in the yellow glow of 200 Watt bulbs across the house popping on. As he continued to look for any intruders, he noticed that the Victorian standard lamp that Sophie always read by was laying on the floor. Mr Nips, their ever-mischievous African grey parrot, had crashed into the standard lamp, an errant grey feather stood testimony to that, and blown a bulb, basically frightening Chris half to death in the process. Letting out a hot breath of relief, he nevertheless patrolled the rest of the house, checking each room, and then headed out to the garden, paying particular attention to the shed. With each step, he thought someone would rise up out of the darkness. Finally, when nothing appeared out of the ordinary, he ascended the well-trodden stairs, now sure he would get to sleep.

What he hadn't seen was the small EpocCam web viewer attached to the willow tree, currently beaming his every move into the cloud, to be viewed at leisure and some length, as it turned out.

Chapter Ten

Beem did not start his day as usual. Today, at 7 a.m., he was already sitting in his office and Google had been humming away for an hour.

Today he had decided. Shit or get off the pot. He would finish as much research as possible, and then sit down with Sophie to decide if they should go to the police. If so, what would his approach be? But first, he wanted some answers; he would then have some context, at least, to base his discussion on with Sophie about what he should do next. It could be difficult to take it all to the nearest police station, having destroyed the original rucksack, envelope, and parcel packaging. He'd also wiped clean all the contents of the rucksack, therefore destroying any evidence that it might once have belonged to another party and not him. He could get five years for being in possession of the firearm, just for starters, and how on earth would he explain the money? Yes, he had also taken some time to clean it, obscuring his prints and other DNA. However, that was really no certainty of anything nowadays with the scientific advances and techniques he would clearly have no idea about.

Some of this logical thought process was his mental support argument for Sophie, who he knew would advise the local police would be the best place to start. However, there was a policeman in the group of photos. Finally, it begged the question why he hadn't reported it immediately. It all looked a little incriminating. Actually, it looked bloody criminal.

This was getting increasingly complicated by the day and he could feel the pressure mounting.

Chris was using the day to review the list and photos via the net. He wanted to be able to share his thoughts in a logical and transparent way this evening, so he had just today to prepare.

The policeman was Inspector Gabriel Raby, the local Traffic Safety Coalition Coordinator, head of the 'kill your speed, not yourself' brigade, and child safety liaison officer for schools. He was easier to identify than Chris had expected – the police normally didn't have a high profile on social media – but the *Lincolnshire Echo* reported nearly every week on his valiant efforts to reduce the number of deaths on Lincolnshire's winding and frankly overused Roman roads.

It must be a hard job because he looked every day of the fifty-two years the photo had stated him to be. Chris had actually found him in the first place by using his date of birth – it was a very easy way of finding someone on Google or Facebook, which the person who had given it to him would know. Chris could do it all in the privacy of his own office or shed; he decided which location to use dependent on the in-house activities and noise level, mainly due to the constant stream of Tilly's school friends. Didn't they have laptops of their own or families to go home to?

The articles were basically nothing but praise for Raby's efforts: a testimonial to his good character; medals for good conduct and length of service; and one for bravery, after diving into the Brayford Pool and saving the life of a small girl who had fallen off her parents' boat. Two hours later and more of the same – a good man, no flaws, no clues.

The clergyman was equally easy to trace, having a higher-than-usual profile. He was the Subdean of the Lincolnshire diocese, The Reverend Dr Noah William Morris-Hargreaves, and his job must have been extremely hard because he looked ten years older than seventy. Maybe it was the fact that he very rarely saw natural light being holed up in the magnificent 920-year-old cathedral, which he soon learnt was built circa 1092. The conclusion: he was a good man, with no flaws, no clues.

There was a very good synopsis with the kind of easy-to-digest facts which tourists knew but lifelong locals didn't, so Chris read it quickly to see if it would reveal anything of interest.

There was a large blurb about the cathedral as it was famous and had its own imp. It sat adjacent to Lincoln Castle which had already been established by William the Conqueror in 1068. Located in the south-west corner of the upper, once-Roman city, this now makes up the historic core of Lincoln, joining the Cathedral Quarter through a Roman arch into Castle Square. It was remarkable what you could get from ten minutes on the net.

He already knew this area well. When he took Sophie out for dinner, they inevitably visited one of the many excellent restaurants along Bailgate or the Strait, up Steep Hill, all luckily available on their doorstep.

He could get nothing of interest on the first two names he had researched and he considered packing it in. Trying to link them or get some insight into why he had the photos was achieving nothing and it was already 11 a.m.

However, he persevered as he still had five hours of his self-imposed deadline to go.

He had just taken a break, getting a coffee whilst stretching his back out in the kitchen, when there was a loud knock on the door. It actually sounded like someone had run into it with a small family car. He quickly went over and opened it and there, outside, was WWF again. Chris studied him more closely this time around. WWF was a man so naturally large, that he blocked out nearly all the daylight. He was also so unnaturally enhanced through work in the gym, along with maybe a soupçon of anabolic steroids for good measure. The man would have to turn sideways whilst doing some kind of limbo just to get through the door, but fortunately for Chris, he didn't look like he wanted to come in. Chris had just a few moments to take all this in, including the faint tattoo on his face which did nothing to diminish the terrifying look. No doubt, that was what he was trying to achieve. The look said: *are you scared yet?* No doubt, that was also why he was here and why he looked the way he did. And why Chris was, indeed, scared.

Chapter Eleven

Chris instinctively took a small step backwards and stood ready for action, but the WWF faux postman simply held out his tree trunk of an arm and offered a small, inoffensive-looking postcard, the type you might send from a holiday if you were still a Victorian. Chris gingerly took possession of the card, at which point WWF slowly turned his massive frame and lumbered, grizzly bear-like, down the lane.

He flipped over the card and all that was written was the word 'LASER' in the usual style he had become familiar with.

He thought about chasing after him and demanding an explanation, but frankly, he wasn't ready for the consequences. WWF may look like half-man, half-ape, all pain, but he also looked like the very, very strong, silent type.

Chris just stared uncomprehendingly at the single word. He stood there, rooted to the spot by the door frame, a trickle of hot sweat slowly running down the side of his face. No one, absolutely no one, had called him Laser since he had left the Marines in 1983. That nom de plume was an echo from his time as a recruit.

It had all started at the Commando Training Centre Royal Marines (CTCRM), Lympstone, in 1972. There, he had been given his nickname, Laser, because it amused his new training team sergeant. Apparently, just hollering 'Beem, fifty press ups' or 'Beem, fifty burpees' or 'Beem, run up that hill with your rifle above your head', hadn't given them enough pleasure. It was presumably more fun for the training team to bellow 'Laser Beem'. It went together nicely which, of course, was the real reason. It was quickly shortened to Laser, for ease when beasting him, and it had stuck.

To be fair, a lot of recruits had gotten quite bizarre nicknames, many for far stranger reasons, like a fellow recruit called 'Shit'. He had been continually muttering it under his breath whenever he got dirty, which was all day every day, so it had stuck. Imagine the derogations the training team could come up with to precede that nickname: Dip, Dumb, Bull, Pig, Big, piece of, and thick as, to name just a few. So, on reflection, Chris was delighted with his not-so-outrageous nickname. It helped that he had been an exceptional shot exceedingly early in training. Shooting came naturally to him. He had won his marksmanship badge within the first five weeks – unheard of until then – and he won the troop shooting trophy by the end of training. So, while serving as a Marine, the moniker was apt and he had revelled in it. However, many years later, towards the end of his service, it brought painful nightmare-inducing memories associated with the role he had played during his professional career. The name alone caused him guilt by association, so on leaving, he had insisted he would no longer be that guy and no one would ever call him that again. There would be no point in reinventing yourself if you hung onto the past. Over the last twenty-three years, no one even knew this name; he hadn't heard or seen it in all that time. Until today. He hadn't even told Sophie this name.

Quickly pulling himself together, without trying to show he was shaken, he quickly scanned the garden with just his eyes. Nothing stirred, not that he could see, anyway. In truth, he hadn't expected there would be anything. Whoever it was had achieved their goal with just that single word.

Once back inside, he closed and locked the door with the bolt and then unbolted it just as quickly. It would cause alarm, along with unnecessary and unanswerable questions from both Sophie, and even more so from Tilly. So, he armed himself with one of Tilly's hockey sticks and placed himself at a strategic angle to the door. It would do no good if they came in armed or, for that matter, if WWF came in, but it felt like the right thing to do.

With his heart pounding and blood pulsating around his ears, he picked up the card and flipped it over. He hadn't even looked at the picture on the front. It could be a clue. His heart leapt again – it was a family photograph of Sophie, Chris and Tilly, taken at the Lincoln Christmas Market early last December. It wasn't one of his favourites as he had his eyes partly shut, but Tilly and Sophie both looked great so they had kept it. It should have been amongst the hundreds of semi-discarded pictures resting in the infamous photo drawer, with all the ones which hadn't made the cut and gone on to be framed or turned into a collage for the wall.

He pulled the drawer a little harder than he had meant so, naturally, it came off its runners and clattered to the floor, spilling the contents. He could have screamed but instead got on with looking through it. After ten minutes he stopped. It was so stuffed with pictures he wouldn't know if one was missing or even if a hundred had been secretly added. He put it back in place and promised himself he would tidy it up soon.

The card had told him enough to instinctively know this was all to do with his past. Was his family about to pay for something he had done in another life?

Chapter Twelve

He had no choice now but to talk this all through with Sophie, but would she understand? It was a lifetime ago. Whoever had sent the messages knew more about his past than Sophie because he had always been extremely careful to keep past and present separate. He had created a narrative of himself which was plausible, raised no suspicions, and best of all, it was for the most part true. But one thing was for sure, he was in deep trouble now, and potentially out of his depth.

He sat there for the rest of the afternoon, running through how the conversation with Sophie might go over and over in his head. The result was always the same – guilt mixed with shame and then panic in the face of losing everything he held dear.

Sophie and Tilly arrived at the same time, which didn't give him a window of opportunity to start the painful task of laying out, for Sophie, not just the facts of the last few days, but some personal history he had never wanted to discuss. And then, finally, the real state of their finances, a subject he had been avoiding for so long it had become second nature to just bury his head in the sand.

Sophie and Tilly immediately dashed upstairs to get ready for the evening. Chris had been so preoccupied with events since finding the rucksack, he had totally forgotten his eighteenth wedding anniversary. They had a table booked at their absolute favourite restaurant in the entire world, Le Papillon in St Paul's Lane, near Bailgate. It was always fantastic food and packed with people they had grown close to over the years. Some were considered friends and none more so than Rob and Pip, the owners, who had always spoiled Chris and Sophie, and now treated Tilly like a princess.

The night went fantastically. Tilly kept not only them but the adjacent tables in fits of laughter. She was a natural comic and a great impersonator. The waitress was a small lady in stature, who loved interacting with Tilly, especially when she did an impression of her shakily delivering wine to the table. Chris had to admit, it was hilarious, to the point he had almost forgotten his troubles.

They strolled home and as they got closer, Chris was again rehearsing the overdue conversation with Sophie in his head.

On entering the lane, he noticed the house was lit up like the proverbial Christmas tree. Every single light was on, including all the security lights and the garage lights. The front door was ajar and music was playing from inside. Normally a stickler for security anyway, but especially in the light of what had happened these last few days, he knew he hadn't left the house unsecured.

Panic reared its ugly head once again. He instantly turned to Sophie and Tilly, shouting, "Stand still! Stay right there!" Shocked by the sheer terror in his voice and his actions, they did just that and stood holding onto each other, too frightened to move.

He raced ahead as fast as his legs and replete belly would allow. Arriving at the totally destroyed front door, he steadied himself for the unknown. He was sure it would be a fight. Racing from room to room, carrying Tilly's hockey stick, he found their house trashed, some windows smashed, an internal door reduced to matchwood and piled in the middle of the room. A mental image of a WWF-raging bull sprang to mind. The emptiness of the house only added to the air of menace which combined with the haunting opera, *La bohème,* booming from his office, making for a dramatic scene.

He felt a dark foreboding at the absence of the ubiquitous sounds of Mr Nips. He raced from room to room – nothing except more smashed chairs, table overturned, ornaments strewn everywhere, some smashed, drawers turned out, no graffiti. It was unquestionably not a robbery; his granddad's old dress Omega watch was still on the mantle next to Sophie's birthday money. He snatched these up and pocketed them quickly. Definitely no Mr Nips.

As he entered the garage which housed his Volvo, his attention was immediately drawn to an A4 envelope wedged beneath the windscreen wiper. He knew even before he was close enough to read it who it was from. He grabbed it, tearing it open.

Jumping off the page was the now-familiar and much-despised neat copperplate navy-blue handwriting. It was just a few simple earth-shattering lines, but it said more than Tolstoy could have achieved in five volumes.

My dear Laser,

You must keep the money; you are definitely going to need it.

Everyone on the list, which I have kindly provided, must die by your hand. I do mean everyone, including the girl. I must see evidence of each and every kill.

The whole list must be completed by June 14.

If you go to the police, I will kill Sophie, probably between your home and the job centre.

If you do not complete the list by June 14, again, I will kill Sophie.

If you get caught before completing the whole list, and just to show some imagination, I will kill both Matilda and Sophie.

70

Matilda first.

Yours Sincerely,

El fin de tu mundo.

PS: Mr Nips (stupid name for a parrot) is in the boot of your V70. Think of this as your first and last warning. Get on with your task. Leave the girl until last.

A cold shiver not so much ran as sprinted down his spine as he raced around the car, finding his keys in the lock of the boot. Remembering his earlier mental warnings of Independent Explosives Devices (IEDs), he very carefully but quickly opened the boot. Inside, with no pretence of hiding, was Mr Nips. More precisely, separate parts of him, bloodied and clearly dead.

If that was not enough to take in, there was a recent school photo taken of Tilly last week, slotted into his broken beak.

He acted quickly, knowing the threat to his family was real, although not imminent.

He had got the message loud and clear.

He rushed to the shed to check if the money was still there. The shed hadn't been touched. He opened the safe, took out the old rucksack, relieved it of £5000 and the gun, placed everything back inside the safe, and then quickly relocked it.

By the time he got back to the front of the house, the girls were standing on the threshold, crying, still holding onto each other for dear life.

He was rapidly running out of workable excuses for his sudden frightening behaviour. He was also in no mood to try and explain that his reckless, selfish, greedy actions had now brought death and potential destruction into their once peaceful and happy lives.

All he could do, in the spur of the moment, was make up a tall tale (outright bloody lie) about burglars. Mr Nips had probably disturbed them and must have taken flight in the commotion.

Tilly wanted to search for her beloved Mr Nips immediately, but it was late, and he managed to persuade her to wait until the morning, buying him time so he could, he hoped, form a better lie. Yes, actually lie to his beautiful daughter – something he had sworn on the day of her birth twelve years ago that he would never do, just as he would never let her down in any way. But it would be the only way to keep her and Sophie safe; he knew that now.

He was in too deep. Whoever was doing this knew too much about him, about his dark history, and way too much about his family and their habits. They had, by design, left him no way out, no loop-holes. When you drink with the devil and all you have is a short straw, you pay the price, the ultimate price if you weren't careful. Well, he was going to be careful from this moment onwards, very careful.

He was resigned to the fact that he was going to kill again, of that there seemed to be no doubt, no way around it. Only this time, the motivation was not for the Queen and country, not following legally issued orders. This time it was for blood, his life-blood, his everything.

He swore a silent oath, one he would find himself repeating like a kind of mantra – he would do anything. Actually, everything. His all and, yes, he would kill for them if it kept his precious family safe. He didn't give a tinker's cuss what the cost to him personally was going to be. He was ready to pay it.

Chapter Thirteen

Chris had only just managed to keep Sophie from calling the police. He had shown her nothing had been taken, indicating it was just mindless vandalism, and minor criminal activities like this are exceptionally low on their priorities.

It wasn't long after they had tidied up, just enough to make the house mostly secure, that an exhausted Sophie turned in.

She turned to Chris and said, "What is happening to us?"

He bit his lip and just shrugged his shoulders. Inside, he was screaming.

Chris had no intention of retiring to bed at all that evening. Racked with guilt, he planned on working on an idea to get Sophie and Tilly away from him and safe, so he could face down what was inevitably coming next.

The first thing he did was to sneak their African grey parrot out of the garage. Taking the precaution of bagging and boxing it, he hid it in the shed. If they found him, it would be the last straw. He'd never get them to safety.

As he did this, he felt even more guilty than if he had actually killed Mr Nips himself, because he knew that for the last three days, he had been trying to find a good reason to keep the money. Whoever had sent the postcard also knew that about him. He was a greedy man who had, in the past, done plenty for money, none of which he was proud of. If they knew that simple detail about him, they knew it all.

Chris spent a long time working on the story. He had

considered telling Sophie the whole truth but that wasn't going to work, it was too late for that. So, he prepared a version that gave her some of the salient facts, just enough to convince her to help with the decision he had already made.

She would go along with his ad hoc plan because she, too, would do anything to keep Tilly safe, and for now, that was all that mattered.

How he wished he had the guts to tell her everything. He believed that eventually, she would understand, and in due course, everything would go back to normal, but he knew she deplored violence of any description. It would also mean really telling her the whole story, the full nine yards, details of the years working in intelligence, then deep undercover, the contract killings leading to his suicidal thoughts, even the mental breakdown which had culminated in his dark moods, his Black Dog days. She had always been there for him but would not have been if she had known the truth about him. He couldn't even contemplate telling her about his 'laser quests'. He had never needed to explain any of this to Sophie. She had always taken him at face value, always loved him for who he was right here, right now. But now cracks were starting to appear in the thin veneer of respectability he had coated himself with for all these years. But he would be damned if he was going to sit idly by and let his life slip through them.

He was now in professional mode, so the story he told was good. Incredibly good, convincing, even plausible. Sophie and Tilly had found it easy to believe him because they both wanted to believe him. He had never lied to them, they knew that, so why would he start now? Well, he was, and he hoped and prayed they would never find out.

The story encompassed some of the real facts, along the lines of: threats of harm made in the night, he had discovered it was a targeted robbery gone wrong, house too insecure. It helped to rack up the paranoia that a spate of violent house break-ins had recently been reported. It would be safest, just, for now, to stay on their lovely houseboat moored up at Looe in Cornwall. Think early holiday. It was, after all, only one day until the official start of Easter half-term, so no inconvenience at all. He could search for Mr Nips, could fix up and repair the house, and then he could join them in a few days and enjoy a much-needed break. He told Sophie that he had recently sold his grandfather's watch. She was surprised and shocked – it was, after all, his only family memento – but he had insisted she would need spending money. Cornwall wasn't cheap, plus there would be some mooring fees to be paid on arrival. He gave Sophie the £5000 to take with her. Tilly was excited at the prospect of going to their boat and readily jumped at the chance of starting half-term a little early. Tilly was a high achiever, so it would not be an issue. Also, her school, like many others, as enlightened educators, considered travel an active learning opportunity.

Sophie was not totally convinced. She had more questions than answers, but with Tilly running around packing and squealing about where they would go first, talking non-stop nineteen to the dozen, where they would need to stop for petrol, what snacks, drinks, what entertainment they would need, she was already planning the whole event – Sophie reluctantly let it go, having fired a verbal warning shot across Chris' bows.

She simply stated, "We will need to have a serious talk when you get down to Cornwall."

He knew what that meant and couldn't agree more. Sophie seemed more relaxed at the simple gesture of him agreeing immediately. He would be relieved to finally tell her everything, absolutely everything, warts and all. Let the chips fall where they may.

He couldn't wait, but as events unfolded, he would bloody well have to.

So, with some relief, Sophie had agreed. She had packed the car, which had taken most of the day, and was a little surprised to find Mr Nips had left a feather in the boot. But she wasn't unduly worried – he was always up to some mischief. She had called in sick for the day, then promptly booked a holiday for Easter, fooling no one. They had not been happy, but were they ever?

With everything which was taking place, Sophie was surprised and more than a little angry because Chris was pushing her away. It seemed to be happening a lot recently, and she felt hurt and scared they were drifting apart. She had agreed to this against her better judgement. She was worried for him, as well, but she would always put Matilda first, so it was a midnight run down to Cornwall. Chris had insisted it would be a better start time, something about the lighter traffic, easier driving late at night with Matilda asleep, a quicker trip. It all made sense, but she still wasn't buying it. In the end, she knew she would have it out with him once and for all, so for now, it was all systems go. "Cornwall here we come," she said to Matilda, with a slight tremble in her voice, feeling like someone had just stolen her dreams.

Chris was relieved; he had managed to get his precious family out of harm's way. He waved them off and watched in solemn silence, with tears pricking at his eyes, as Sophie's blazing taillights faded into the distance, beginning their six-hour trip to safety.

He was not the only person watching in solemn silence, although she was 150 miles away.

Chapter Fourteen

Lucia also had tears pricking her eyes, but these were of pure joy at the havoc she was witnessing. She had been spending many a relaxing hour watching Christopher go about his daily routine; she had particularly enjoyed watching the guilty look with which he had taken the bait she had left for him to find. It had not mattered which route he had taken on April 2, he would still have found a blue Puma rucksack. Every possible route had one similarly placed to look like it was an accidental find, and a good stroke of luck for Christopher. She had been messing with his business for over a year now, so when curiosity made him peek inside and see a couple of £20 notes 'accidentally' left in the top compartment, coupled with the teasingly placed five £20 notes, which had painstakingly been placed in the now locked zip, he would have no choice but to take it home. And sure enough, he had. It had taken her team over an hour to retrieve the other rucksacks. She was not worried about the money, but she did not want any of the other guns falling into the wrong hands and being used for nefarious purposes, possibly harming an innocent – except the ones she had planned for Christopher. She was not a monster.

It had, however, been of the utmost importance that it should be April 2 when this all started for Christopher. It was equally important that it came to a successful conclusion on June 14. These were milestone dates for her, and the significance would become painfully clear to him soon enough. For now, though, she was amusing herself by dropping a few subtle hints and a couple of little clues here and there. The 'Puma' rucksack, with its very distinct colours, was just one she had come up with in the jet on the way here. She felt sure he would cotton on sooner or later, but it did not really matter either way. She had seen his reaction upon receiving the letter spelling out exactly what he was going to do. He was now in play and would be right up until the very end.

It was only at that moment she decided that he may, after all, need some extra encouragement, or maybe she would need some extra leverage. She picked up one of her brand-new gold-plated iPhone 5s and dialled a pre-set number. The phone was answered within two rings, as she knew it would be.

She relayed her instructions, without doubts or second thoughts, in fluent Štokavian. Not her mother tongue. She had recently learnt the language because she knew what she needed to get done could leave no room for interpretation. That was how misunderstandings had turned into tragedies for her Bosnian and Croatian employees.

They knew all too well that if they did not follow her instructions to the letter, especially as most of them were detailed and complex, it would not end well for them. A few had just vanished. Privately, some had even begun to complain that this was worse than being in the army, even during the recent war! But since '95, they had had no choice but to work for the highest bidder, and Lucia made sure she was always that person. Now she was making good use of them, despite the occasional fatal misunderstanding.

For now, she was content to watch Christopher tangle himself deeper and deeper into her web. *"Oh, what a tangled web we weave, when first we practice to deceive."* How right, she smiled.

Chapter Fifteen

Chris drew a deep line in the sand, figuratively speaking. This was it, it all had to stop. His girls had been gone for only a few minutes, and he sat at the dining room table, rereading the letter, with its clear direct threats to both Sophie and Tilly. It made his blood boil to the point he had to physically calm himself down just so he could get on with planning his next actions. Whilst he must continue to identify the targets on the list, that much was clear, he must, in equal measure, find who had sent him such an uncompromisingly brutal message. What on earth had he done in the past to bring such fire and brimstone down upon himself and his family in the present? On that score, he still didn't have a clue, but the dates in the letter told him it was connected to the battle for sovereignty over the Falkland Islands way back in 1982. My God, that was thirty years ago, and while some things were etched in his memory, most of it was forgotten. He had buried them deep in the annals of time, forgotten as they should be. But the who and the why, for him, remained a mystery for now, something he was determined to change before he lost it all.

He decided his only starting point for the who was probably the what, and the what was WWF. He was the only link to the real villain of the piece who had thrown down such a dramatic gauntlet by killing Mr Nips and issuing vile promises. They were no longer threats, that much he knew.

Most importantly would be the who. Finding them would allow him to end this quickly. He was adamant he would not be doing what had been demanded in the letter – he was no longer that person.

He also knew he would need help – no man was an island, after all – and in the Marines, it was the team in teamwork which kept everyone safe. The same could be said for the laser quests – those well-paid little excursions to foreign lands. A soldier of fortune, if you will. Well, for a fortune anyway. Maybe it was with that in mind which had made him subconsciously keep a shortlist in his little black book of some very serious expert military types. He now knew he was going to need to call in some very big chits sooner or later. Sooner was his guess.

Chris decided to prioritise the only tangible piece of the puzzle – WWF. He didn't know anything about him, apart from his shaved tattooed head and massive bodybuilder's frame, and a postal uniform which looked three sizes too small. It was like his super-sized muscles seemed to be making a concerted bid for freedom and he was about to explode out of the shirt. Well, you didn't get that size unaided. A serious gym habit combined with a serious steroid habit would be Chris' guess.

So, he grabbed his laptop and searched for the type of gym that WWF would need. He was looking for places where he could sling some serious iron, so only ones which had free weights, and a lot of them. WWF could easily lift a car and probably his house as well! He thought WWF would probably be from out of town, so he may only have guest membership locally. This could take some time.

It was only a week since he had found the rucksack but he already felt the pressure of the looming deadline hanging over him like the Sword of Damocles. Despite that, he still believed (he really did) that he had no intention of following through with their demands. However, he knew he had better get started before he got any nastier surprises. He really needed to get to them before they could get to him. Again.

Total Shape, Health First, Grid Iron, Gold's Gym, Mr Mussel! No, really, Mr Mussel! Even meatheads had a sense of humour – or couldn't afford the repainting job! Well, you get what you pay for, right? Lloyds, Big Bench and the Y, which was actually the YMCA, although he was pretty sure there was no way WWF was going there after the Cowboy, the Builder, the Indian Chief, et al. Overall, there were a dozen gyms and six in total had free weights. A few phone calls, with him pretending he was the Incredible Hulk who needed real weights for real men, no juice bars, no latte bars, just power bars and dumbbells with big dumb guys to help him in his quest to be the biggest man in the known universe, narrowed this down nicely to three. Now, he would have to join them or pretend to join. Actually joining might lead to doing himself a permanent injury.

Chris needn't have worried on both accounts – finding WWF or pretending to work out. He found him in the first place he tried, Gold's Gym, which was a well-known place for the serious iron-slinging he-man… He could see for himself it was a bodybuilder's paradise, no doubt about it.

WWF was, as he had suspected, a serious ironhead, meaning whilst he was in the zone, you could have nuked him and he wouldn't have noticed. So, the fact that Chris was studying him, looking for any signs of weakness, also went completely unnoticed. A couple of hours later, WWF was pumped enough to compete in the Mr Universe – hell, he was pumped enough for even the Mr Intergalactic – bodybuilding competition. He was finally – without showering, Chris noted – ready to leave. WWF packed his energy bars, power drinks, weight belts, gloves, and lastly, his personalised sweat vest which read 'Pain is for

Pussies'. Charming. It brought back a flash of memory showing Chris he was no better. Whilst training with the Special Boat Squadron in Poole, he had worn a badge which had read 'no sea too deep, no muff too tough'. He'd never worn it in public, though, not after the beasting he had received after having been seen by the commanding officer's wife while out diving. Lesson learnt; time to teach one to WWF.

WWF headed for the car park and squeezed himself into what looked like a toy car. He was actually sitting on the back seat, an impressive piece of contortionism. God help him if he ever needed a quick exit.

Chris followed on his mountain bike (Sophie had the car; he would need to get a hold of another one soon) by actually being in front of him. He kept just enough distance ahead so he could see him in the handlebar mirror. Most people who suspect they are being followed look over their shoulder and WWF was no exception, despite having great difficulty rotating his average-sized head on distinctly unaverage, massive, oversized shoulders. He did double back and change route several times, but as bodybuilders are noted for the size of their arms and not the size of their brains, this didn't cause Chris any problems. It helped that Lincoln's road traffic was a nightmare due to the introduction of one-way systems along with, to his advantage, cycle lanes with purpose-built pedestrian parts. Eventually, WWF led Chris to a high-walled, gated, multi-storey, detached house on the edge of the St Catherine's area on the outer-city limits. It was one of the few houses in the area which had its own palatial grounds. An impressive structure, which was more fort than a town house. In the low evening light, some of the upper floor's lights were on and he could see, in one of the windows, a strange-looking cloaked figure.

Chapter Sixteen

The enormous electronic security gates were very slow in closing, allowing Chris to slip through easily. He quickly and quietly searched the grounds around the edges of the building, looking for any obvious threats. He also looked for escape routes, both for himself and WWF. He took note of the registrations of the two cars and noted the features of the mountain bikes which were chained up. He spotted the CCTV cameras, together with the night vision cameras. He saw the pressure sensor pads' indentations along the drive and path and the motion sensors along the neatly manicured lawns. He realised this was far from just casual surveillance. As with the gates, these were heavy duty, more for protection than just a deterrent. *What could they be protecting?* thought Chris. That's what he was there to find out. Upon careful inspection, he found a secure blind spot near the lower-level exit. As he was about to enter, he placed, under a pile of left-over bricks, the handgun and silencer which was now loaded and cocked ready. Ready for what, Chris wasn't entirely sure. Answers were his profound wish.

The exit door was sealed tightly shut so he gingerly crept around the building only to find the massive ornate front door was not locked. Perhaps WWF wasn't expecting anyone to slip in behind him; perhaps he really was all brawn and no brain. Nevertheless, it was an invitation he could not resist. He considered going back to retrieve the gun, but experience had taught him a couple of things. If you carried a gun, you could end up shooting yourself in the foot, or it could be used against you, so no protection there. On balance, he decided to leave it where it was. If they fired at him, he would then feel obliged to retrieve it and fire back. However, he was sure they wouldn't be firing anything at him; they had, after all, given him a job to do. He would not be the one to start anything; he was here for reconnaissance only, not to start a fight. He now lowered his profile and looked through the opening at ground level so he would not create a silhouette against the frame of the door. He thought he could just make out a figure lit up in the gloom of the interior, a woman, perhaps wearing a black cloak, maybe sitting at a desk. She looked like she was far away, sitting at the end of a long oak-panelled corridor. The fabulous-looking grand entrance contained many ornate marble statues on either side and a sturdy brass umbrella stand. Its contents might come in handy later, he thought.

In fact, unbeknown to Chris, the woman in black was indeed very far away, 150 miles to be more precise. This image was courtesy of a state-of-the-art webcam and was being beamed out of a very impressive 80-inch high-definition TV monitor.

"Do please come in, Laser," said a voice, sounding somewhere between a purr and a threat, with an accented sinister edge.

"I have been waiting for you," echoed around the corridor.

Shit! thought Chris, a little too bloody late. Well, a lot too bloody late. A trap which, of course, had been one of the many scenarios he had entertained but quickly dismissed. This was more like a baited hook, with WWF being the bait.

He was pleased he had left the gun hidden outside because the entrance was one massive metal detector, very much like the ones you saw in the entrance to a crown court building. Another reason why they had no need to worry about him bringing the gun, which they had kindly provided – using it against them would be just too poetic for words.

He might not be physically armed right now, but any single object, innocent to most, could suddenly become a weapon for self-defence, or offence, to someone well trained in unarmed combat, which he was.

He had taken no more than six cautious steps into the long corridor when suddenly, out of the shadows, emerged WWF like a menacing black cloud with a look of sheer hate plastered across his granite face. It told Chris all he needed to know: WWF was devilishly quick and quiet for a man of his size. This was not going very well, and this was going to hurt.

He surprised WWF, though, by remaining completely still, poised, looking, listening, sensing, while WWF charged at him full steam. With only a split second before the hammer blow of a punch landed, Chris swiftly shimmied to one side and grabbed WWF's wrist, pushing it towards him and slightly upwards. Usually, the natural reaction would be to grab hold and hang on for dear life, but not this time. Just as the arm gained a 60-degree angle, exposing a vulnerable part, Chris smashed the onyx ashtray from the nearby table-top smoking set into WWF's exposed elbow. It had the desired effect, smashing both the ashtray and the elbow into several pieces with an added bonus of stopping WWF in his tracks. This gave Chris his next opening. He stepped to one side and snap-punched WWF in the left ear, giving him a painful ringing in his ear but also pissing him off. WWF reached out his gorilla-like arm and grabbed Chris by the throat, lifting him clean off the ground as effortless as lifting a cream cheese bagel to his oversized mouth, which by now contained an oversized grin.

Chris had to react quickly as the vice-like grip was getting tight and he was already seeing stars. Fortunately for him, he had been well trained at great expense, but not so WWF. His training had stayed with him all these years later. However, he had never imagined it would be used to escape a 6 foot 7, furious 400 lb World Wrestling Federation gorilla. Grabbing WWF's thumb – just one thumb, that's the trick – with both hands (which he needed, because it was like grabbing the leg of a thoroughbred racehorse: all muscle), he then snapped it down with every bit of power he could muster as quickly and as hard as possible. The effect was immediate. WWF let go and Chris dropped to his knees, punching WWF in the groin as hard as was humanly possible. This, thankfully, had the desired effect and WWF crumpled to his knees, letting out one almighty scream. Well, he would have let out a scream, if Chris hadn't delivered an accurate, hard (but not hard enough to break his own wrist) blow to the now open, right-side hinge of WWF's firm angular jaw-cum-temple, thus rendering him both screamless and unconscious.

Chris sprang to his feet, quickly looked around for other assailants, and finding none, he dashed down the corridor towards the woman in the black cloak. As he moved a little closer, he realised she wasn't in a black cloak, she was in a black box, a massive TV, and she was smiling, a smug little self-satisfied, tight-lipped, uneven smile.

Chapter Seventeen

Lucia sat quietly fuming to herself. Her alarm had sounded during a structural renovation of the house's old cellar, so she was in her working outfit – a navy-blue, pinstripe, Prada two-piece suit, but still a working outfit – no makeup, with hair like a bird's nest covered in chalky plaster dust. It could not be helped, she supposed. She had not wanted this but she could not wait to see Christopher live, as it were. However, it also had the advantage of giving away nothing about herself.

Lucia patiently sipped a 1947 Chateau Lafite Rothschild while she waited to see the outcome of the ongoing fight between Christopher and Mladic, her Bosnian Serb employee who she called B4. They all had remarkably similar-sounding names, making it difficult for her to keep track of who was who, hence they became B1–B10. Two had, over the last twenty-four months, failed to make the grade, so she only had eight of her little B's remaining. Plenty for the task in hand, her little project.

She was sitting comfortably in her palatial London townhouse, a little unhappy that Christopher had found her Lincoln house. She had made it very comfortable and extremely safe at great expense. Again, it wasn't the money, it was the time which had now been wasted. She had intended to use it as a secure base, a safe house with a built-in prison if it came to that, which she was sure it would sooner or later. The timeline for her move north had been in just a couple of weeks so she could be closer to Christopher while he worked his way through her Kill

List. She had wanted to see the death and destruction for herself, up close and personal. Also, if Christopher had to be killed, she wanted to be there to look him in the eye and tell him why.

It would also be more pleasing to give her little B's orders one to one. She wanted them to see and feel the passion in her eyes. Money and threats alone would not be enough in the end. She was sure they all understood the importance of this whole venture, not just to her, but to them. Failure resulted in missed opportunities and missed comrades.

Christopher finally beat that idiot B4. She knew he would. The man she had hired was only there for his appearance, a visual message. Now, he was expendable, easily replaced. He had served his purpose and she hoped Christopher would kill him. It would save her the trouble.

He would not see B1, B5, and B8 coming, that was certain. They had, after all, been watching him for eleven months already.

Chapter Eighteen

Placed in front of the wall-mounted TV was a black leather, comfy-looking chair which she offered to Chris with a simple sweeping hand gesture. He decided it was prudent to take it. He needed the rest after his first fight in twenty-eight years. Now, perhaps, he would find out who she was and why this was happening to him.

He could see that she was a very smart lady, possibly in her middle to late fifties. She could have been a lot younger and had probably once been extremely attractive. But there was no disguising that she now looked worn around the edges, sort of shabby chic, without the chic. Her whole appearance was suffering from the benefits which a high-definition TV provided. He thought about mentioning this but chose kindness over point-scoring. This was not the time for banter, witty or otherwise.

Her nose was so far out of alignment, that it looked like Michael Jackson's plastic surgeon had tried to fix it and given up halfway through. She also had a horrendous scar under her left eye, so deep you could see where the plastic surgeons had tried, really tried. It had silvered with age and stood out against her once smooth olive skin. The unfortunate effect was to give the eye an absurdly angled, very wonky appearance. Her nose was also slightly to the right of her oval face, producing an odd asymmetrical, off-balance look. 'Mad-Eye' Moody from the Harry Potter books immediately sprang to mind. It did, however, give her the benefit of the fact that even the slightest smile had an evil appearance, something she must have worn for nearly all her life and now she didn't even notice.

He was surprised to see her still calmly sitting there, just sipping red wine. *Mad-Eye Bitch,* thought Chris. The only sign she was real was the annoying malevolent, come-and-get-me smile playing across her thin lips. The smile didn't reach all the way to her eyes, not even the good one. Mad Bitch, indeed.

He was still getting his breath back and taking in her unusual appearance when she finally spoke.

"Laser! That was not very nice." She spoke in a low gravelly voice with a slight Spanish accent.

"How do you know my old service name?" he enquired.

"Quiet. QUIET!" she snapped. "I will speak, you will only listen."

Chris decided it was better to listen – it may be to his benefit. Two ears, one mouth and all that.

She continued, "I do hope you have not hurt him! He is very precious to me." Again, smiling a sinister-looking, tight-lipped smile.

"I only wanted him to deliver you a message *before* you get started on the list I have provided."

Chris was sure she chuckled for a fraction of a second when she said, 'before'.

"I gave you all that money for such a simple task, which clearly you are more than capable of."

"But I didn't ask for any of this," Chris tried to interrupt.

"I told you to be fucking QUIET!" she screamed at the top of her voice. Her whole head twitched for a fraction of a second before she quickly regained control.

"Let me spell out what your next move is. You kill everyone on the list within the ten week deadline. You now only have seven and a half left, or your wife and daughter will die, make no mistake about it." She paused for dramatic effect, which worked because Chris was too stunned to move or say anything.

"I will not tell you that again. Oh, and you will not find us so easily next time, so do not waste any more precious time trying. You will not enjoy the consequences. You may leave now."

Finishing her monologue, she began to rise out of the expensive-looking seat, still with the red wine in her hand. She was still wearing that annoying little 'I-know-something-you-don't-know' thin-lipped, evil-looking smile.

Chris was so stunned by the calm, matter-of-fact monotone in which she had delivered such a threatening message that he didn't immediately react.

He was still shaking with adrenaline-filled rage as he jumped to his feet, ready to shout and swear, to question her sanity. But she was right about knowing something he didn't know because at the very instant he was on his feet, there was a little flicker of a movement just visible out of the very corner of his eye. He turned only just in time to see a massive anvil of a fist, presumably belonging to WWF. It connected with the whole of his face and, without a single sound, he dropped to the floor, unconscious.

Chapter Nineteen

Chris regained consciousness, feeling like he had been run over by the bulls in Pamplona, to find he was locked inside a toilet cubicle, presumably the gents beside Lincoln's south common. Being a known haunt for men to meet like-minded other men, or so Chris had heard, this was not a place to be caught with your pants down. The now-empty handgun was dismantled, clean and recently oiled, by the smell of it. It was lying at his feet on a plain brown leather cloth, the fifteen 9 mm rounds were in a neat row on the toilet roll holder, looking like critical little soldiers. Next to the silencer, there was also an envelope tucked underneath his right shoe, yet another reminder of what a fool he had been.

Nothing was going to be gained by staying where he was and there was everything to lose. This turn of events had set the clock well and truly ticking now. He rushed outside, gratefully finding his mountain bike locked to the rack. The combination was, as he feared, 381. He really must change that. He dashed home.

After showering, he cleaned his cuts, dabbed some frozen peas on the bruises, grabbed a coffee, washed down a handful of paracetamols, and with his head clearing, was once again sat at the dining room table. He opened the letter which contained a single A4 sheet in the now-familiar style.

My dear Laser,

Well done on finding me so quickly. We were expecting you but not for many more weeks. The residence is now completely empty so you will find no further clues. Who I am, and my reason for demanding you personally eliminate the six people in the photos will remain a mystery until I decide it is time for you to know.

I do feel my investment in you is well placed and I have every confidence you will be successful.

Please do not waste any more time on me. I am but a minor player in the scheme of things. It would be better for all if you could now concentrate on the task at hand.

I wish you all the best in your task. Please see the evening news.

Yours Sincerely,

El fin de tu mundo.

PS: I hear Cornwall is lovely at this time of year.

With his hand shaking, he grabbed his mobile phone and pressed speed dial 1 whilst simultaneously turning on the TV. The call went at once to voicemail.

Hello, this is Sophie B. Please leave a message after the tone. Beep. With his heart in his mouth, he calmly left a call-me-back message. Then he quickly rang Tilly's mobile; it was a recent gift for her and he hoped she would have it with her, and remembered to keep it charged.

Hi, this is Matilda's new mobile phone. Beem me a message. Beep.

He did not leave a message, but he did slump to the floor, doing all he could to stop a full-blown panic attack from kicking in. He sat on his hands to stop himself from punching the wall and throwing his mobile across the room in anger.

He called Avis, packed what he needed to get to Cornwall, and was ready as quickly as was physically possible. Right now, he wished he had installed the phone on the boat, as Sophie had asked for last year. Mobile coverage was spotty at best so he hoped it was just a poor signal because her mobile just kept going to voicemail and so did Tilly's. He eventually left messages on both, casually asking for a return call as soon as possible so they could catch up. He didn't want them to see the missed calls and worry. He didn't seriously expect a reply soon; there had never been a mobile signal anywhere in Looe town and the locals had banned a mast in order to keep the authentic little fishing port looking, well, authentic!

He had already decided he would dash down and move them. He would have to tell Sophie the truth but that was the least of his worries. It was a race against time and one he must win.

Just then, a news bulletin reported a renowned London-based European bodybuilder and convicted drug dealer, Mladic Petrovic, had been found dead on the back seat of his car in Lutterworth, Leicestershire, from what appeared to be a drugs overdose. An Interpol arrest warrant was still outstanding for war crimes, the news reported. Chris sat there, stunned, trying to absorb the news that WWF had been killed simply because he had led Chris to their Lincoln safe house. If nothing else, it proved beyond any doubt that they were both ruthless and efficient. It also meant that MB – the mad bitch – was the business, authentic, the real deal. They were serious – this was no joke.

There was no way out of this, not that he had, against all hope, believed there would be. All this had taken money and years of planning to set up, to set him up, and MB was going to get her money's worth, that was for sure.

While he impatiently waited for the hire car to be delivered, he considered the problem. At no time had he ever been in control of the situation. Every turn, every move, they had expected, even anticipated. They knew him, knew how he would think. Only someone who had either been in his position or had known him thirty years ago, would have this level of knowledge. They must also be watching, which gave him a new challenge. How could

94

he continue to try to find out who was behind all this while he was still assessing the targets for elimination, or indeed, actually eliminating them? How was he going to get his family safely out of harm's way whilst remaining unseen? He realised he was repeating his oath under his breath. He would do anything, literally anything, he would do everything physically possible to keep them safe. Yes, I'm sorry to say, even kill. He realised the shocking truth of that fact was that it didn't bother him, not one bit.

He knew he should be mortified by that simple truth, especially after all this time out of the game. He had been in any number of life-threatening situations pursuing legitimate sanctioned targets, so he knew the cost, both on him and them in turn, but he had never expected, even in his wildest nightmares, his family to pay the price.

He was quickly reverting to type, returning to his former state. Not father, not husband, not successful businessman, but an assassin.

No, no, no, not again! he thought, but here he was, and time was not his ally. He would have to get back in the zone very quickly.

He took out a Letts A2 notebook and set about outlining his next steps. It would have to be like a military operation. Select a target. Unfortunately, he had two – the list and MB – and that was one too many.

He was going to need help.

Select the ground. He would have to recce each target individually, and that would take much longer than the seven weeks he had left of the deadline.

He was going to need help.

Select the most effective method. The small pistol would not be enough. He wanted to be able to kill effectively over a longer distance, with a greater chance of getting away.

He was going to need help.

Select the best weapon. He had an idea forming that he hoped would achieve the 'how' when it came to the Kill List.

He was definitely going to need some help.

So, he was using an old adage, make a plan, test the plan, adapt, and overcome.

Normally, in the operational list of tasks, number one would be to select your team but he no longer had that luxury. He did have options, though; he knew at least one person he could call on for help, someone who would never let him down.

He relaxed at the idea of taking back some control, but the very moment he let his guard down, he immediately started to worry about whether he was going to lose all he had worked so hard to get – a loving family, peace, sanity and a sense of really belonging. Was it being snatched away? It was.

But not if he could stop all this in its tracks.

Thirty-five minutes later, part one of his plan was taking shape. The rental had arrived, not before time.

He would begin to put his plan into action. First, he would secure his girls, then he would research all the photos and learn all he needed. He would have to find out who MB was and what her real motive was. It wasn't his death. They had proved they had the discipline, they had proved they were more than capable of killing, so what was the unknown agenda and why was he just as much a target as the entire list?

Right now, he was going to get his girls back and put them somewhere even safer. He headed out of the lane and set off to get his life back.

Chapter Twenty

He drove as quickly as he dared and did everything in his repertoire to make sure he wasn't being followed. Parking up on a long-isolated stretch of road where he could see for miles in all directions, he scanned the horizons through a pair of high-powered binoculars for hours. Once he was sure, he headed directly southwest.

As he drove, one glaring fact became apparent over and over again – he couldn't do this alone. He would have to become part of a team, just like in the good old days. Everyone had an important role to play during any successful mission, and experience had taught him that a strong support network was worth its weight in gold.

Chris decided it was time to ask for help. He knew it would be forthcoming, no matter what was asked, providing he asked the right people, and he knew exactly who to start with.

He was going to move his beautiful girls to a safer location, yes, but this time with protection, armed protection.

He continued his roundabout route, constantly changing direction. He wasn't taking any more chances. Just before dawn, he finally found himself on the A38, a few miles outside of Exeter. He had decided he must make a little time to stop off and pay a flying visit to one of his oldest and dearest friends, despite not having seen him for twelve years. He drove into Exwick and parked several streets away from Sketchley's house, which was a two-up two-down in a shabby, you wouldn't look at twice, street. Sketchley had got his moniker from the recce troop lads of 42 Commando, thirty-five years earlier. It transpired his then soon-to-be-divorced wife had left him whilst he was on deployment, removing everything of value and cleaning out their joint bank account. She had her solicitor draw up a settlement which had placed a fifty per cent charge against his wages, directly into her account. Once he had returned to Bickleigh Barracks, he told everyone that she had taken him to the cleaners. Everyone had laughed and, eventually, so had Sketchley. Sketchley's was a national dry-cleaning chain at the time so, inevitably, his moniker was born and had stuck, but had at least been shortened to SK. It seems, from what Chris could gather from the messages in the Christmas cards, it had happened on more than one occasion. The nickname had stuck because the wives hadn't.

Chris couldn't wait until 08:00 to be sure SK was up, he just didn't have the time. He quickly walked the three streets, pretending to call into several houses so he could be absolutely sure he hadn't been followed all the way from Lincoln. He was sure.

Sketchley opened the door and without so much as a "what the fuck are you doing here?" or "what the hell time do you call this?", he rushed out and bear hugged Chris until he could hardly breathe. SK then manhandled him into the front room, slamming the door shut with the heel of his combat-booted foot. SK was one of those former Marines who had had a difficult time letting go. Even though he had left the service in 1991, he was still wearing khaki combat trousers and a khaki green mountain survival shirt. Along with his black combat boots, he looked like something out of *Dad's Army* – balding crewcut grey hair and a paunch which Jockey Wilson, the dart-playing legend of the 80s, would have been embarrassed to be seen with. He sat on the period settee – which period it was hard to guess, but the 1960s would have been Chris'. He accepted the proffered black coffee which miraculously came with a bacon sandwich, brown sauce, and all.

"So, what brings you back into my life, Captain?" Sketchley started.

"Oh, please. It's Chris," said Chris.

"Okay, Chris, what's the problem? I assume it's not a social call? For that, you would have at least called first," continued SK.

"Okay, okay! I'm sorry! It has been far too long but I really do need your help and you're the only person I trust. It's not just for me, my old friend, it's for my family," responded Chris, quickly.

He didn't waste any more time. He quickly brought SK up to speed, leaving nothing out. This man had seen and done everything you would expect of an experienced, highly decorated sergeant major in the Marines. Often alongside him, he also had Chris to thank for his life. It was not something they would speak of today but the memory flashed across his mind while SK was making some personal arrangements. He and SK had jointly served in Northern Ireland when he was a sergeant and SK a lance-corporal. It had happened during a routine foot patrol which had gone very wrong indeed. He quickly let the memory dissolve; he was not in the mood to reminisce. He laid out the first part of his somewhat sketchy plan. Such as it was, Chris would go and get his girls, and meet SK later today once SK had secured the location Chris had in mind. SK made a quick call, there and then, and without any hesitation at all, simply said, "I'm in, Captain." Old habits died hard for SK.

Grabbing his motorcycle helmet and keys, he already

understood the urgency. Also, for no apparent reason, he had his kit bag packed, ready to go at a moment's notice. Maybe he was heading towards his fourth divorce.

SK headed straight off towards Okehampton, thinking through the mysteries of his life. He was indeed heading towards his fourth divorce; his wife of only two years had left him just a matter of months ago. According to Anna, she loved him, she said he was kind, caring, sweet-natured, but still, the divorce papers cited his inability to let go of the past. He had even kept his stupid bloody name! It was all true. He had tried time and again to become a proper civvy; he had worked at it, he'd taken meaningless jobs, or thankless soul-destroying tasks, but his temperament, coupled with civvy life's lack of natural leadership and structure, had sapped his will. It had drained him of his spirit and his once abundant courage. Civilian life was something he just couldn't come to terms with. Leaving his beloved Marines after twenty-one years was like a bereavement for him; he missed it all. All the time.

He had even tried therapy to stop his life from just ebbing away. The therapist had called it institutionalisation. This, coupled with PTSD and his natural inclination to sweat the small stuff, made him a square peg in the round hole of the ill-disciplined, self-centred, naturalised civilians. It was the uniform which gave him structure, discipline, and order. She had told him to apply to the police, and he would excel there, but SK thought it was all just too late.

So, when Captain Beem had just turned up out of the blue, it was like manna from heaven. He was back doing something he loved, for someone he loved, protecting his team from everything the outside world could throw at them. He would insulate them from harm. It was his watch again and everyone on it would be safe. He would keep Sophie and Tilly safe and out of harm's way. It was now his sworn duty, an oath he was happy to make; he would be happy to lay down his life to keep them safe. After all, he felt he had nothing left to hope for, now or in the future. Laser had once again saved his life.

Chapter Twenty-One

Chris continued his journey to Looe, a perfectly formed little fishing village on the Cornish coast. He was more determined than ever to make sure Sophie and Tilly were safe before he could even consider the next part of his, and now gratefully, SK's plan.

He parked the hire car two miles away in Millendreath at the Cove Inn. He was sure he wasn't being followed but paranoia was creeping in, so he felt he had to make sure. He ran along the cliff tops which overlooked the North Atlantic Ocean. It was a beautiful part of the English coastline, and this route gave him the opportunity to continually check he was not being followed. Just because you're paranoid, doesn't mean you're not being watched. Under different circumstances, he would be in his element, but he was focused on a different task – making sure his family remained safe.

He quietly slipped into Looe via the east beach which was fairly busy for the time of year with families enjoying the sand, not the sea which was too cold, building sandcastles, or simply strolling along the amazing seafront towards the harbour.

He passed his V70 parked in the harbour car park. It came as a massive relief to see it; it was a good sign.

The harbour was packed with fishing boats, most abandoned or rotting, many of which had been transformed into floating homes. Only a small amount still worked at bringing fresh fish to the idyllic port every day. He casually strolled up the pier to Mooring 23. It was there he had his prized houseboat. It had been adapted from one of the local fishing boats which he had been given as payment for some work developing a retired fisherman's 'Nautical But Nice' fishing memorabilia website. It wasn't a very big fishing boat and made an even smaller houseboat, but they all loved it so it was a favourite destination for their family holidays. He had worked hard one summer to convert it to a twin berth, with the roof and foredeck being transformed for al fresco entertaining, an open-plan functional dining room with a galley area which led nicely onto the poop deck and open-plan seating area. He had also fitted a jet-ski ramp which had always been so much fun. He smiled at the thought of Tilly asleep in her hammock, swinging gently in the breeze on the poop deck. As an infant, she would only sleep in a hammock. She had insisted on it, but only if her dad would sleep with her. She would scream her newly developing lungs out, until he would reluctantly, but not too reluctantly, give in and sleep in the cold, uncomfortable hammock. She always got her own way from the very beginning. She had her dad wrapped tightly around both her little fingers and he would not have it any other way.

As he climbed over the handrail, coming on board, he first noticed the table and several deck chairs were on their sides. Not particularly unusual when you had a teenage girl always running around. But then he noticed the door was slightly ajar and that it had an angry-looking crack running across the glass pane from deck to roof. He could see, even from a few paces away, that the lock had been forced. His heart pounded in his chest, while at the same time it made his blood run cold, ice cold! Fear tightly gripped his stomach, making him feel sick. His throat was constricted with fear – it was like trying to swallow a golf ball.

He dashed, tripping headlong into the bridge, scanning, searching the boat's every nook and cranny, but as he feared, he came up empty. No Sophie, no Tilly.

It looked like an almighty struggle had taken place. There were a few spots of blood on the floor and a splatter of blood across the starboard porthole, like a string of red pearls.

Chapter Twenty-Two

He found the distinctively styled handwritten letter almost immediately. God, she did like her little mocking notes. It was taped, by one corner, to the middle of his 45-inch TV hanging on the wall beside the galley table.

My dear Laser,

Forgive me, but did you really think I would let you squirrel away such beautiful assets as Sophie and Matilda, just bobbing around, a life on the ocean waves?

Laser, you are clearly not sticking to our agreement and this causes me great pain.

Whilst visiting me at my Lincoln house, only yesterday, did you not learn anything? I am omnipresent, all-pervasive, ubiquitous. I see all.

'SHE IS FUCKING GOADING ME, NOW!' Chris shouted aloud, punching the TV in anger and frustration, reducing it to a small pile of electrical waste.

I know everything about you, I know everything about your family, and I know you will do as I have asked.

If you have any last shred of uncertainty about your task, I suggest you please look in the fridge. You will understand my displeasure is genuine.

I like to share my pain; they say a pain shared is a pain halved. For me, Laser, pain is to be savoured.

By me... not you!

Yours Sincerely,

El fin de tu mundo.

PS: They were having such a lovely time…

Chris tentatively opened the galley fridge with a shaking hand. There, to his horror, he saw it contained only one item. Sitting squarely on the middle shelf was a small silver tea plate on which sat a 6-inch square block of aspic. Floating in the middle of the aspic, contained within, was something which at first glance looked like a carrot suspended in mid-air. On closer inspection, he saw it was a small human finger. He quickly realised it was a ring finger complete with rings, both engagement and wedding. He could still see the scarlet nail polish.

He knew what it was, knew who it belonged to. The realisation exploded in his mind like fireworks on Bonfire Night or the Fourth of July. The room started to spin and his ears rang like the bells of Lincoln Cathedral. He had to steady himself just to stay upright but he didn't manage it. He slipped to the floor and wept.

With tears stinging his eyes and a deep dread in his heart, he contemplated the possible state of Sophie. She was still alive, of that he was sure, or it would have been her head in the fridge. He did not dare to even think about Tilly. It broke his heart, and he could not get past the mental block he had raised as a defence mechanism, or he would just lose his mind.

Why hadn't he come straight here? The guilt threatened to overwhelm him, rolling over him like his very own emotional tsunami.

He stayed on the floor, with the fridge lighting up his already blotchy tear-stained face, and cried a little more. Not a manly, shoulder-shrugging, quiet cry, but a full, tear-spilling, snot-dripping, howling cry from deep within. What had he done?

Not having time for self-pity, he regained his composure quickly. He would get answers, such as why they wanted him to do this so badly. How had they found the girls? How many resources did she have to be one step ahead, right across the country? Why set up such an appalling image inside the fridge? Why had they gone to so much effort to make him kill? Who hated him so much that they would mutilate his beautiful Sophie, or even worse, kill her and Tilly? He couldn't help himself; he sobbed again.

Just as he was getting up from the floor, with all these questions swimming around in his head, and still sickened with the terror of these events, he saw another unwelcome, handwritten note, neatly weaved into the rungs of the lower shelf.

God, no. Not more torture.

My dear Laser,

You should have heard her scream, and the terror in Matilda's eyes was a sight I personally will not forget in a hurry. Well, hopefully not. I did tell you I liked to share the pain.

You have taken my money. So, I took your family.

You know what happened to my messenger 'before' you could get within an inch of me.

I will video their painful deaths so you will be able to watch them over and over, knowing it was all your fault.

Do not worry, I have no intention of killing you. Your suffering will be eternal. You really must get a move on. Be careful you don't get caught too soon because next time it will not be a cut little finger. No, next time... neck.

I will not be writing to you again, you just do not have the time, so I have set up two untraceable 64-bit encrypted yahoo e-mail accounts.

Your address is: laopossum@job.com.ar and the key is

62584381.

My address is: lapampas@job.com.ar.

They both have unlimited capacity and triple lock encrypted cloud storage. Simply send yourself a message. It will automatically BCC to me and vice versa, making them untraceable, which means there will be no evidence if you are thinking you might use it against me. I know you are a clever IT boy.

Laser, I promise to give you the time. I know it will not be easy to complete the list without getting caught. Your family will remain safe and be completely unharmed but only if I see progress is being made. They are resting in the lap of luxury. They have rooms of their own, including en suite facilities and even a daily maid.

The deadline of June 14 is, however, just that, a 'dead' line.

Use the e-mail fast, or the next notice you get will be a funeral one.

Yours Sincerely,

El fin de tu mundo.

PS: I had intended to post another card but you made me kill the messenger.

PPS: I hope we do not have to send any further encouragement to you. It would cause me great pain, but even greater pain for Matilda. And for Sophie, it would, however, be deadly!

Chapter Twenty-Three

They do say, no military strategy or plan survives first contact with the enemy. It was never truer than right now. He needed a new plan of action, a survival plan for him and his family, one which now included getting his girls back safe and unharmed.

But he just couldn't move. He seemed to be stuck to the deck with shock and fear-induced adrenaline. He felt drained with fright and confused. Why had it all gone so very wrong?

It was a simple plan. First, hide them, then move them to safety with SK, who was the very epitome of an experienced bodyguard. He would have made sure that all Chris lived for stayed safe, leaving him free to execute his part of the plan and hunt down MB, because, after all the threats to his family, he didn't want to kill anyone on the 'list' more than he did her.

MB had foreseen this move and was still one step ahead, back in the driving seat. Importantly, she was showing him how absolutely ruthless she was. He understood that there were no empty threats in any of the handwritten notes. MB had enjoyed writing them, he was certain of that. As for the finger, if WWF hadn't been warning enough that time was rapidly running out, aspic on a plate certainly hammered that home.

Chris slapped his face to focus his concentration and decided he could only do as MB demanded, so he would head back to Lincoln with a small detour to see SK. Time for a new plan, and one which would work for them against MB. For it to work, they would need even more help.

He had texted SK saying he would meet him at the agreed destination, only he would be coming alone. He saw the Volvo keys in the conch shell and picked them up. He was going to need the estate car now.

He rang Avis as he power-walked to the East Beach car park and told them where to pick up the hire car. He had already placed the keys on the little hook located deep in the passenger side wheel well which Avis had placed there for a convenient driverless handover.

Setting off in his Volvo, he was pleased to see that it, for once, had a full tank of diesel. The one-hour journey took him three, having taken time to make sure he wasn't followed. He didn't want anyone to know he had already secured himself some very experienced help.

He arrived at the now disused Okehampton Range and Training Camp, without headlights so as to approach unseen. He and SK had both spent many months here as training safety instructors for the Marine recruits' final commando test. The thirty mile yomp across Dartmoor in eight hours or less had been dropped in the mid-80s due to health and safety.

He walked the last mile and was relieved to see SK. Dartmoor was a bleak place, even in the summer, but at this time of year, it always reminded him of a scene from *The Hound of the Baskervilles*, with its low-lying fog creating its own eerie, soundless atmosphere. With SK beside him, he felt a wave of calm sweep over him like a warm blanket. The images of a real plan started to appear from his battered and emotionally bruised brain.

"What the hell went wrong?" enquired SK the second he was close to Chris.

"How did they know Sophie and Tilly were in Cornwall? Is

your house bugged? Did you sweep for electronics? Where are they now?" SK enquired.

"I really don't know, but they must have had a listening device in the house. The plans were made at short notice, and they had only been there a couple of days. I don't know where they could be now, SK," was all Chris could say with his head in his hands.

"But I'm bloody well going to find them, no matter what the cost," Chris whispered.

"And so am I," reassured SK.

They quickly sketched out a rough plan, in several parts. Chris would, indeed, carry out their demands of killing everyone on the list, which he would do without a second's hesitation – it was the only way he was going to get his girls back. SK would recruit some trusted old comrades to hunt down MB and her team. He was sure there would be more than one WWF lurking in the shadows.

"I've got your back while you do whatever you need to do. I will help with all the detail, trust me. I will not let you down," was all SK could think to say.

With a hand on his shoulder and a small lump in his throat, Chris reassured him. "I know that. I've always known that."

"I do have one idea. If it's feasible, it will be a lifesaver. I'm going to see Gunny," Chris stated flatly. SK didn't even think about contradicting him.

The years of experience which came with his steady rise through the ranks had taught him many things. The delegation was one of the first. No one could do every aspect of any operation, especially when leading from the front. There was always someone who could do certain things better than you, much better. Knowing when to let them, was the trick.

111

Finding MB was going to be no mean feat, but he had known SK during his time in Recce Troop 42 Commando, then 14 Intelligence Company. There, SK had been the troop's colour sergeant and intelligence coordinator. He had proven to be one of the absolute best at find and capture. Chris had seen this first hand while he was head of long-range tactical over cover, forward operations Northern Ireland, in the spring of 1976. SK, who always had a keen eye for detail, was always vigilant, but most importantly, he was patient. He possessed many years of experience, covering all types of tracking, which was invaluable in finding even the most elusive IRA members, even tracking a senior lieutenant to a cattle farm in the south of the country. He had eventually found the cunning bastard hiding in a midden, in full scuba gear. He had risen silently with his plastic-covered AK47 aiming directly at the back of SK's head, but he didn't get the chance to pull the trigger because Chris had pulled his own trigger, and with that, the IRA lieutenant had sunk quietly back into the abyss. The shit had nearly hit the fan that time.

If you had to rely on just one fellow human being, SK was that man. He gave Chris an edge that MB would be unaware of. SK would be able to bring a skill set to the party that Chris never could, and he also had a great black book of useful, in situations like this, old comrades. One of the reasons he hadn't seen any of them for countless years was that they had never been in a situation like this, and never really thought they would be ever again.

SK was secretly glad to be in this situation once again and had no more doubts about himself or his worth to society. He was doing again, in the thick of action, instead of just remembering.

Chapter Twenty-Four

Lucia sat comfortably, smiling to herself in her favourite rustic, white leather Fritz Hansen egg chair, which was in keeping with the rest of the room's décor – minimalist.

The call with Christopher had gone better than she had hoped, at such short notice, after the fool B4 had led him right to her front door. She would have liked more time to prepare for her first face-to-face with Captain Beem.

She was happy to be back in her main UK home. She had only been in Lincoln a short while, inspecting the house and making sure it was ready. She did hate wasted trips, which this one had so drastically been. Here, she was always more relaxed. She sipped her 1928 Macallan 50th anniversary Malt Whisky, savouring the unique balance of flavours. It made her smile to realise it had cost, at a private auction, more than the Lincoln house, which she had only bought as part of what she called her *little project*. She loved this house. It offered her a level of comfort, a level which she had, over the years, become more comfortable with. It allowed her to relax for the first time this week. She sighed and set down her crystal tumbler next to the portrait of her adored late father and headed down to the basement. Once again, she was dressed in a navy-blue pinstripe work outfit, only this time, she was made-up and looked her resplendent best.

She had the help of B9 and B10, who were actually Vymdin and Vdin, respectively. The B numbers both helped her to remember, and was belittling to them, an added bonus. Within the basement, there was also a very strange looking, small, wizened, dark-skinned, crumpled fleabite of a woman who was constantly moving. She seemingly only possessed a single tooth in her whole mouth which she kept continually licking as though she had a polo mint stuck on it. It was her nervous tic. She knew to be nervous; it was this nervousness which had kept her alive all these years.

The little woman kept speaking in rapid Spanish, annoying Lucia, who hissed into her ear, *"Callate la boca, Juanita, si Ella muere ella muere,"* at the top of her voice. "I do not care. Now, be quiet, for once in your miserable life. *Por la boca muere el pez.*"

They had transported Sophie and Matilda from Cornwall in the back of a customised Mercedes van, which had no door handles, lights, or seats and was also completely soundproof, arriving at her safest of safe houses; this one was in Mayfair. It had once been the Argentinian Embassy but had for a long time been in private hands – hers.

Sophie and Matilda were hooded, wearing a soft ball gag and had their wrists bound. They lay, quietly slumped on the cold, hard, concrete floor. They made no noise, partly due to shock, partly due to abject terror, but mainly due to the sedatives.

Lucia removed their hoods. She was not concerned about being identified. She had an escape plan back to South America, and her destination had no extradition treaty with the UK, which was rather pleasing.

Leaving the mouth gags and the plastic cable ties in place, she had B9 and B10 frogmarch them further down the recently modified cellar, closely followed by Juanita.

The cellar looked both cavernous and empty, but on reaching

the halfway point in the room, they were steered into a secret doorway. This passage led further underground, giving the impression that it went on forever. Eventually, Sophie and Matilda were shoved through another doorway and into an equally massive room. In there, there were two purpose-built wire cages. Each cage contained a brand-new memory foam mattress, an ablutions bucket with a toilet seat, a small square of a Persian rug, and an industrial-sized, galvanised length of steel chain. The chain was approximately six feet long, with old-fashioned metal handcuffs, the type with a corresponding sister key. They were impossible to pick; Houdini himself could not get out of them. Juanita gently attached these to Sophie's and then Matilda's ankles, then equally as gently, the ball gag and wrist ties were removed. The cage doors were then firmly locked with Squire maximum security, closed shackle padlocks.

Lucia sat on the only piece of furniture in the whole cellar – a comfortable-looking Charles Eames lounge recliner. It was a £950 replica, so she was not worried about its location. Once she had lit a cigarillo, she studied Sophie first, then, in turn, Matilda. After a satisfyingly long draw, she expelled the smoke out of both nostrils simultaneously, like a bull about to charge. Even one of her eyes had an animalistic twinkle in it as they searched every inch of her new, long-term captives.

Lucia called Juanita to kneel beside her. She did so immediately, cowering like a whipped dog. With her entire body, Juanita silently pleaded for Sophie not to speak, not to move, and if possible, not even to breathe, for she knew extremely well how Lucia hated to be interrupted. The stripes etched into her back stood testament to that.

"My name is Lucia Maria Domingo. I expect you would like to know why this terrible thing is happening to you?" began

Lucia. The slight accent had an obvious Spanish ancestry. "If you do not interrupt me and keep Matilda from continually crying, I will tell you."

"Do not look at me with such disdain, Sophie. It is all your husband's fault; he started all this by murdering my precious father and I am going to finish it. Then, I am going to finish him. If you behave, both you and Matilda may well live through this ordeal, but only if you do exactly as I instruct."

Sophie held her bandaged hand. The morphine was wearing off and the sedatives they had been given this morning were also less effective. Without thinking, as an involuntary reaction, she cried out in pain and despair for her and her daughter. It just tumbled from her lips before she could even try and stop it. In a whisper, she beseeched, "Why us? Why us? Why, why, why?" The tears were now falling freely down her dirty, blood-stained face.

Lucia jumped up in a sudden rage which sprang out of nowhere. It spread across her face like wildfire. Her good eye rolled around manically while she punched the air, close to being hysterical.

"I said do not interrupt, and keep your noisy fucking daughter quiet or I will be forced to. You had better believe me when I say my kind of quiet and yours are stellar opposites. Mine is a lot more permanent," she raged.

Sophie was so shocked. She had barely spoken a handful of words. She calmed Matilda as best she could but they both shook violently. They were too petrified at the sudden outburst of pure hate to really manage to remain totally still.

Lucia stood for a minute, calming herself down with the help of Juanita who soothed her from a distance; she knew it could be deadly to get too close during one of these attacks.

Lucia regained her composure remarkably quickly and headed towards the almost invisible door, simply saying, "Get comfortable. She will feed and water you. I have a husband to terrorise – yours."

Sophie and Matilda were left in the dark, still completely in the dark.

Sophie did not understand any of this but from the way they had mutilated her hand, and from what she had just witnessed, she knew for sure Lucia was totally mad.

She knew she was unlikely to get any answers from her, but maybe Juanita could be persuaded to help. She had seemed genuinely concerned for them. There was also something in the way she looked at the mad bitch which gave Sophie some cause for hope.

Chapter Twenty-Five

Chris and SK had spent a long night reworking their plan. They left Okehampton camp at separate times and in different directions, both agreeing that with what Chris had in mind, SK must remain a secret. They would need the element of surprise or it could go horribly wrong.

It was raining hard when Chris traversed across Dartmoor. The only signs of life were the bedraggled sheep, which seemed to live on the grass verges despite the beautiful mass of rolling hillside and small outcrops. He knew from bitter experience that this was often an extremely boggy landscape. Many sheep had died in this hard terrain or had drowned in the fast-flowing streams, fallen foul to the unseen dangers of the life-sapping bogs. He had once heard a story that a whole Chieftain tank had been lost to the bogs of Dartmoor and he believed it. No wonder the sheep stuck to the edge of the road, it was at least for the most part a hard surface and one he was happy to travel along.

He quickly found himself at Bodmin, the geographical end of Dartmoor and the beginning of what looked like the real world instead of some scene from a Hammer horror movie. As he drove along the A38, he prepared himself for his next stop. He was not feeling confident with the small pistol he had been given to do the job. He had a feeling he would be needing more firepower, so he headed to Exmouth to visit a former US Marine who had also been a Navy Seal, and had worked with SBS. That's where Chris had met him. He had even spent a brief period in the French

Foreign Legion. Towards the end of his active career, he had completed tours of Chad and Iraq in the guise of a fully paid-up mercenary. He was sure to have, or at least be able to get, even make, what Chris believed he would soon be needing.

His name was 'Gunny'. Well, his real name was Kevin Smith so it was no wonder he preferred Gunny.

Chris arrived in Exmouth at dawn. He knew exactly where to go but was not in the mood to take any chances, so he parked at the railway station and walked to the seafront. He then walked its full length and climbed the steep cliff at the northwest end, continuing on for about thirty minutes before finding himself back near the start point, all the time making sure he wasn't being followed. He crouched to kneel and wipe the sweat off his brow and thought all this evasion hadn't done him much good recently, but what he was going to need from Gunny was not strictly legal. Well, actually it was illegal, so he took no chances. He didn't want anyone to see him there.

Chris arrived at the rear of the two-storey townhouse and after a short pause, he slid over the back fence and landed on all fours, cat-like. He waited a short while before standing up. SMACK! Bang. Wallop.

He awoke on the fake-leather settee and gingerly opened his eyes to see Gunny standing in the corner with a can of Strongbow in one hand and a half-smoked Cuban cigar in the other. He rose gently. The room was by now full of acrid smoke just hanging in the air like a grey ghost. He gave a couple of involuntary coughs, more out of seeing the smoke than actually tasting it. Gunny just continued casually looking at Chris and then said with a broad New York accent, sounding like something out of the mafia, "What the fuck? Buddy? I could have shot you."

Chris sat up and accepted the proffered can of cider; he knew he would be needing it. He was about to relate a long, if fairly unbelievable, story. He would need to convince Gunny to help while making sure he could convince him he wasn't dropping him in the shit. Gunny was allergic to all things official, like the law or taxes, but once you had him on your side, he would do anything for you. Chris would have to tell him everything, or at least as much detail as he believed was required. Gunny ran with some very unsavoury types these days, according to SK. Chris told the story of the last couple of weeks. He also had to give him a potted history of his life since they had last met, outlining why he hadn't been down south since the last Falklands reunion he had attended in 1992.

"The fuck you say? That's one hell of a story. Are you shitting me? Because it sure sounds like it." Gunny was good with guns, and bad with grammar.

Chris reassured Gunny he was not telling porkies or indeed exaggerating in any small way. In fact, he'd left out the part about the finger, for Gunny, with all his NY hard-man persona, happened to be one of those types of people who fainted at the sight of blood. Gunny could feel dizzy at the mention of it, a strange phenomenon for a battle-hardened former US Marine! Still, he did know his way around just about any weapon you could name. More importantly, he could adapt or build you a weapon to any specification, including the pair Chris was now desperate to get his hands on.

Gunny took Chris down a flight of stairs. Then he took several minutes to unlock a steel door which looked like it could withstand a nuclear explosion.

Once inside the room, it opened out into a workshop that Bosch or Siemens would have been proud of. The room contained every piece of equipment which an arms manufacturer would need to start World War Three, or invade a small country, at least.

Chris and Gunny sat at a drawing board while he outlined what he wanted – desired range, dimensions, specific characteristics, portability, the specs he thought he would need, along with the rounds, which would also have to be handmade. Gunny would fill in the blanks and calculate the exact dimensions to make it work, the first time, every time.

All this bespoke work was amazingly only going to take a day or two but was going to cost £47,000 cash. Gunny might have been an old comrade and long-time friend, but business was business. Chris paid him without hesitation.

Captain Beem was once again going to get his very own sniper rifle.

Chapter Twenty-Six

Chris took the time to clear his head and mentally review the plan while he drove home from Gunny's. He had taken the build time to catch up on much-needed sleep in the gunsmith's spare room; Gunny had spent that time making some detailed drawings and by the time Chris was ready to leave, he had nailed the design specifications and the technical aspects of the rifle, overcoming some real physics of the physical challenges along the way.

Chris drove on towards his destiny but for the first time in two weeks, he was happy that with the help of SK and maybe a few additional highly skilled resources, they could make it work.

It had to.

The one pressing and currently unanswerable question was the police. How could they possibly stay one step ahead or hope to remain liberty intact? This was an important challenge. He needed his freedom to be able to keep his girls safe, which was more important than any laws he was unquestionably going to break. He knew, with this kind of attitude, he would never solicit even an ounce of help from the Old Bill. They would simply lock him up, throw away the key and call it a job done. It would be a tricky balancing act that he was going to have to perform – one slip and it was a disaster. He thought that if he positioned things well and was honest about his real intentions, he might, just might, find this missing piece of the puzzle and ultimately survive it all.

He set his mind to neutral and mindlessly ate up the miles.

He didn't want to spend a single second contemplating the fate of his beautiful girls. He was a mile past Leicester, on the newly completed dual carriageway, when he became aware of his surroundings again. It had only recently been opened, so he had to concentrate, but this led all the way to Lincoln, shaving forty minutes off his journey time. The improvements to the highway were well overdue, a welcome relief from the usual massive hold-ups on this once single carriageway.

Chris went straight home. There was no reason to hide his intentions here, quite the reverse. He needed to let whoever had kidnapped Sophie and Tilly know he was completing his tasks as requested. Getting on with 'the list' was now, he believed, the only way he could affect a quick and safe return of his family.

He reversed his car into the garage and shut the doors, taking out the shopping – not the sort you could buy at Asda, more important than that, much more important, especially if the next seven weeks were going to be successful.

He then went into his office with no great expectation of being interrupted or disturbed, but he still, for only the fourth time ever, locked the door.

He lifted the lid on his laptop, booted it up, and thirty seconds later, he was on Yahoo and setting up the e-mail account. It was straightforward and once he had typed the address and set the password it was done. He typed in a short message to let MB know he was going forward as instructed, simply sending: *watch this space*. On pressing the send button, the words dissolved into a random pattern of numbers and hieroglyphs. Without the corresponding key, you would never be able to break the code, even if you worked at Bletchley Park and owned your very own Enigma machine.

He then stowed one of the fishing rod-like cases under the

stairs with seven near-identical fishing rod-like cases which actually had fishing rods in them. The wood for the trees, he smiled.

Next, he took the vastly improved L115A3 all-weather sniper rifle, the tactical rifle that Gunny had modified for him at such short notice. It had proved the most consistently accurate in any terrain for marksmanship, with reliable strikes from 2.47 km, or 1.535 miles, if you prefer. Gunny had used some custom parts from other specialist sniper rifles. It had become apparent that Chris' idea for the customisation of the weapon had already been under development for peacekeeping purposes, so the leap in technology had not been that dramatic. What had been more dramatic and made this weapon special was the handmade, purpose-built, one-of-a-kind rounds. These were utterly unique, hence, the price tag. He had only received twelve but he was sure he could make that work for him. Just in case, he had asked Gunny to provide ten more, as backup. Better safe than sorry, and he didn't care about the money any more.

He took the rifle apart and broke it into its three constituent parts – lock, stock, and barrel. As he had requested, it came apart effortlessly. It was also quick and quiet. Firmly securing them into a hard-shelled, locking banjo case (said banjo now being wall mounted as a failed musical experiment), he placed it just under the office desk.

He then set about completing the research he had half-heartedly started so many times, only this time with real purpose, focusing totally on the businessman once High Sheriff, Connor Laurence Mercer, 61. Eight hours later, he had everything he needed. Planning and executing raids had been one of his former specialisations, along with his ability to shoot. The only missing part was an alternate rendezvous point, a safe location if anything went wrong. Mainly hiding from the police, was his first thought. Three hours later, he had the perfect place which he had dredged up from somewhere in his memory bank, at least he hoped he had.

He also hoped and prayed, to any God who would listen, that MB was going to be true to her word, and until at least June 14, his family really would be safe and comfortably sound. He knew this was not going to be easy, and it was not going to be a quick operation. He let those thoughts linger for a just a moment, savoured them, and just as quickly as they had arrived, he let them dissipate. He knew he would not have any available energy for unwanted emotions.

On the outer edges of RAF Waddington on the outskirts of Lincoln, just past a lovely village called Bracebridge Heath, were some abandoned wartime ammunition magazines. They had originally stored the munitions for wartime Lancaster Bombers and latterly, the Vulcans. These outbuildings were grassed over, arched concrete, Nissen hut, and bombproof shelters which disappeared into the landscape, all linked via deep underground tunnels.

Chris had led an exercise in 1980 to check the security of the UK's RAF bases, including RAF Waddington (it was the memory of this that had brought him back to Lincoln to live), in the light of renewed IRA attacks taking place on mainland Britain. The exercise was to test the security and preparedness of the RAF Regiment should they be a target. It was well known that these bases were vulnerable, often open to the public with easy access for plane spotters and terrorists alike. During one of these evaluations, he had come across this abandoned set of bunkers. He had noted that their location, whilst inside the secure perimeter of the fences, sat well over a mile from any aircraft or fixed structures. Consequently, they were marked clearly on all MOD maps, so the official report just noted them as abandoned.

On his mountain bike, Chris had slowly cycled past the bunkers several times today. He was incredibly pleased to see they were still there and even more overgrown than thirty years ago. He had endured an hour or two of plane spotting, in an appalling red wig and homemade fat suit. He wasn't so much worried about MB, but the RAF still had observation posts along its perimeter and he didn't want to alert any eagle-eyed sentry. He would need a closer look at the bunkers tonight, so he headed to the Blacksmiths Arms in Bracebridge Heath, which sold very good pub grub along with a decent range of beers. He opted for Lincolnshire sausage Toad in the Hole, mash, and onion gravy, which was excellent, accompanied by a Bass shandy.

He ate the meal in peaceful silence, as he had taken the additional precaution of leaving his phone at home. He had long since suspected that MB was using it to track his movements, not through some sophisticated spy software, but by simply using the good old 'Find My iPhone' app. It was a feature on all his family phones, good for locating everyone but bad for hiding from determined stalkers. He also changed into a recently purchased tracksuit. New, shrink-wrapped clothing couldn't have any tracking devices sewn into them. He was going to get a hand scanner tomorrow; SK had located one. He didn't ask where – you never did with SK. Sometimes it was better not to know.

He had also swapped his mountain bike for an old diesel Moto Guzzi motorbike, borrowed – well, secretly borrowed – from a guy at the allotment, which was going to be an especially important part of the plan. As the abandoned base would play a key role, too, it was essential that he wasn't followed, so he took extra precautions before finally arriving at the Nissen hut magazine labyrinth. He used an infrared torch, which could only be spotted from a distance of a few paces. From the state of the undergrowth (which was actually overgrowth – no one had been here for an exceedingly long time) he could see there was no one around. Well out of sight of anywhere (except above, and even he would notice a drone), he located a double door entrance far away from the road, in the middle of the huts. It had an excessively big, extremely rusty lock, holding the lever handle in a secure position. This, in turn, secured the lever bolts, top, middle, and bottom. This would have been tight security in its day, as you would expect. He left the locks well alone. Leaving them in the same condition would not arouse any suspicions from a casual observer. Instead, he worked on the far side door, gently lifting the very rusted hinge bolt which basically crumbled away in his hand. Repeating this exercise with the middle and bottom, he then simply moved the whole thing on the axle of the nearside hinges, opening the whole double door, security levers, rusty padlock and all, away from the frame. No damage, no noise and best of all, no signs of entry. It was completely resealable, so once a new set of hinge bolts had been made to look like a complete rusty set, it would be job done. He would be able to come and go completely unnoticed and it would provide a safe base for operations.

Inside, he was amazed to find the lights still worked. Just a small part of an enormous electricity bill and clearly overlooked for decades, their loss was his gain – the first bit of good fortune. The second came in the form of purpose-built ammunition cages, which could be locked. But the pièce de résistance was running water – actual drinkable running water. He thought it was a colossal waste, but he wasn't looking for any gift horses in any mouths right now. This was the perfect place for his plan to work, and not before time.

He texted SK with the grid reference and a description of their good fortune and met him in the Blacksmiths Arms car park the next night at 1 a.m. He had with him the new old-looking bolts which had taken him most of the day to secure. SK had brought with him some items he needed to help him prepare the place as a secure base of operations; they would be needing it in the extremely near future.

They used the anticlockwise route to their new RV, and were able to park SK's recent acquisition in an abandoned farm lane, completely unused for decades. Situated right next to the RAF base fence, adjacent to the magazine entrance, their fortune with this site was reassuring to them both. It was the present which just kept giving – unseen from the road at the end of a small zigzag, just giving and giving.

The next day was the start of the third week since finding that bloody rucksack. All prep was completed so he was going to start the job of working his way through the list in earnest. Setting out the next morning at 5 a.m., he took a circular route around the city for his own safety. Sometimes he moved at speed, sometimes very slowly, always looking and listening for any signs of being followed, monitored or recorded. He avoided areas with known CCTV camera coverage. Yesterday, he had dressed in tourist clothes – three-quarter length shorts, an '*I love Buffalo, Texas*' sweatshirt, sunglasses, and a Bulls baseball cap with an overlarge peak – and spent the afternoon taking what would appear to be holiday snaps. In reality, these were digital images of all locations, both obvious and covert, for CCTV – official, shop, or home security coverage – on roads, paths, grass verges and walkways. There were hundreds of ways of being secretly observed and filmed, for the record, being kept for posterity or a criminal trial! Which was what he was trying to avoid – you didn't get away with killing someone without trying.

He wanted to be able to freely come and go without arousing any suspicion or drawing attention to himself, for when he succeeded in his task, all hell was going to break loose in Lincolnshire.

MB had selected Mercer.

Mercer had easy access for Chris, and as a first run at this, he needed something straightforward to cut his teeth on. Another good reason to begin with Mercer was that he lived locally in Cherry Willingham, a small, very pretty village northwest of Lincoln, which was easily accessible by foot or vehicle. He chose foot. Just over an hour and a half later, he was in the village.

Chris walked casually through the village, now dressed as a farmhand in a blue boiler suit, black wellies, and a very grubby flat cap. He had, slung over his shoulder, an old satchel containing a scope, a video camera, and a pair of powerful binoculars. He was also carrying what looked like a potato sack but, in fact, held the rifle parts, the top and bottom halves of his ghillie suit, three litres of still water, ten energy bars, and the US tourist get-up. After all, he had no idea what to expect or how long it would take to recce Mercer.

An hour later, he was on the other side of Cherry Willingham, heading towards the Mercer bungalow on the edge of the village in the northwest corner. It was conveniently located next to a field of cows; the cattle noise would mask any movement or accidental noise he might accidentally make. Not that he was planning on making any such mistakes; he had recently been rehearsing, bringing back his training, once forgotten, but now a matter of life and death.

He continued out of the village and walked up the long lane

of a local farm, looking like any local farmhand and so raising no suspicions. He found a spot at the rear of the old sheds, a few feet behind a huge broken rusted plough, which was going nowhere in a hurry. He found a dip in the field along the hedgerow which gave natural cover. Through thick hawthorn and wild ivy, some bramble entanglements made it look like the briar patch from Peter Rabbit. For him, it was perfect, a direct line of sight to Mercer's bungalow, who was first on the Kill List.

Chapter Twenty-Seven

Beem lay cold, wet, and hungry, quietly dozing. His senses were still switched on, despite the fact his eyes were closed. He awoke with a start when he heard something he hadn't planned for, hadn't even considered – a bloody farmyard dog, like the junkyard version, only more loving and useful around the farm during the day, but equally as vicious at night, very territorial.

Chris remained as still as possible, hoping his natural body odour would not give him away. He had rubbed himself from head to foot with localised foliage and mud found at this location to disguise his normal scent. The dog was loose and roaming the farm, patrolling his little bit of turf. Chris could only hope and pray it had worked, so he waited and waited. 10:30 p.m. and at last the dog was called into the house for din-dins. The farmer's wife had shouted "*Patch*" so loudly and with such venom, it had made him spring to attention along with the dog. Having made him jump was good; he would need to move fast to get out of there, which he did. He was just coming to the end of the lane when he heard the dog barking back in the yard. He wouldn't be using this yard again. *Patch*? The soppy family-style name had only just registered with him. Maybe he had overreacted, but the lesson was learnt.

He went the long way around and crossed the field opposite Mercer's house. At 12:17, he settled back down in the dyke, in the same spot he had prepared early in the evening. It had, by now, dried up, offering a great natural trench and vantage point.

The dyke gave him an unobstructed 180-degree view of Mercer's bungalow so he settled down for what might be a long night, dressed in full head-to-toe camouflage, cocooned within the overgrown blackberry bush and brambles. He knew that unless someone actually walked along the dyke itself, he would never be spotted. Just to prove the point, someone had actually urinated within a foot of him, which he thought was taking the piss a little.

While he was killing time, so to speak, and to keep his mind occupied (he wasn't yet used to long hours of non-activity, including inducing an almost coma-like state of non-being) while he waited for the flawless kill shot, he thought about the lovely little hamlet that was Cherry Willingham. Its long history could be traced back to Roman times but presently it boasted the amenities which any modern man or woman needed, including some shops and two pubs. There wasn't really much else outside of the primary school which was set in a small dip in the land and surrounded by large, cultivated fields, some with rapeseed, some with cows or sheep, but all well maintained with neat hedgerows, and clean, clear lanes leading to and from the village centre.

Putting these thoughts out of his mind, he looked through his binoculars. He could tell Mercer was on his computer from the flicker of blue light which was creating a strobe effect on his now illuminated face. He stayed on the computer until 3:20 a.m. What was a 63-year-old doing on a computer at 3:20 a.m.? Maybe his accounts, business plans, authoring a novel or just a silver surfer? Well, he didn't care about all that, it wasn't really why he was here. He was here to shoot Mercer, because his family was at risk and that would always take priority, no matter what the consequences.

He remained vigilant all night, staying in the same spot until, at 8:15, Mercer came out the front door, got in his car, revved a little and headed off towards Lincoln. He must be going to work.

Despite his hunger, Chris decided to wait, rest up, and see what opportunities came this evening. He was keen to show MB some results of his actions, but not at the cost of getting caught. That would be equally as disastrous for him as it would for his girls. Softly, softly, catchy monkey.

The evening came very slowly but Chris had learnt patience and had no problem remaining alert and calm.

Mercer returned home at 4:31, looking none the worse for his day's labour. He seemed to repeat the previous night's activities right down to working at his computer until 2:46 a.m.

Chris stayed in position, observing for another hour before retreating the way he had come, leaving his gear in position. He would be returning shortly. He stalked across the field, coming around the rear of the cottage where, from his observations this morning, he knew there were no security lights or CCTV set up anywhere at the rear. He would not be overlooked from any angle. He had also checked whether either Mercer or his neighbours had infrared detection. They hadn't, why would they? Mercer looked like your average guy in the street, your average Joe nobody. He melted into the shadows of the brickwork and slid around the building to peek through the window. Mercer was asleep on a cot in the room, right next to the computer, like he was protecting it. Chris crawled to the door, making good use of his past experience; it was all coming back now. He marked in his book all the details needed to make the shot a first-time success.

Once he was back in the trench, he reviewed his notes and was confident that part one of his plan was underway and would work well. While he had been at the front door, he had left a small electrical device which would ring the bell on command. Chris set up his recently renovated rifle, checked the mercury in the scope was still level, and positioned himself ready for his first shot in anger in decades.

He centred himself – the confidence in his ability was slowly returning – took manual control of his breathing, and checked the wind, the distance, and weather conditions. He knew these elements would not affect this shot, it was too short, but he still took all the time he needed to enter the zone. Finally, fully at one with his muscle memory, he knew he was completely ready. He had one final check on the surroundings – no late-night dog walkers, joggers, cars passing the lane end, or most importantly, no local police patrolling their little bit of turf. Confident he was now ready, he remotely rang the doorbell and waited.

In what seemed like minutes, but was in fact only ten seconds later, he rang the bell again. This time there was movement. The door gingerly opened without any lights being turned on, which didn't matter to Chris. In fact, that's what he had hoped for. Mercer held the door open just four inches and poked his head out of the gap just a fraction, looking surprisingly nervous for your average Joe nobody. Maybe it was the lateness of the hour; maybe he had been caught doing something he shouldn't, like cheating on his taxes. Who cared? The small gap was all Chris needed. He softly caressed the trigger. First position, pause… breath… hold… hold… just as Mercer was in the process of closing the door, Chris silently fired. Phut! The whisper of death.

As he did so, he remained in place a fraction or two longer than he would normally be expected to, with the rifle pointing at and lingering on the shot. This was so he could simultaneously record the high-definition video, using the HDV600 videoscope night-vision camera. This was how he captured the direct hit into

Mercer's chest, one inch to the left and one quarter up from his heart, in all its gory glory just for MB.

Mercer had instantly fallen backwards into the unlit hallway, letting go of the door which slowly closed and finally shut, leaving no sign of life in the small bungalow. In the small village of Cherry Willingham, no other resident of this old Roman settlement could have possibly guessed that Connor Laurence Mercer, the respected High Sheriff of the City of Lincoln, had just been reduced to a dead heap on his own hallway floor.

Chapter Twenty-Eight

Chris packed all his gear including the new expensive video camera. Quickly retracing his steps from earlier, he was once again at the rear of the bungalow from where he easily and silently broke in through the patio doors. Time was of the essence, so he quickly headed to the hallway where Mercer lay. He checked his life signs then, satisfied, sat against the wall, blew out a relieved breath, and sent a text to SK.

He was, after all, going to need help removing the body. SK arrived in a Skoda Octavia electric estate. It was silent and spacious, with an easy access boot, and silver-tinted rear windows, and it was stolen just a week ago by SK in Devon.

SK, being ever industrious and inventive, had sprayed the new addition to the operation in the local Skoda dealer livery so it wouldn't look out of place as it dashed around the county roads. It also had genuine plates and was taxed and insured so wouldn't be stopped, providing he followed the Highway Code to the letter; only the vehicle identification number – the car's fingerprint – would give the game away, but this was totally obscured under the thick part of the windscreen wiper. Bad design feature, but good for SK.

Chris and SK easily loaded the body, which had been wrapped in the hallway carpet, one; to remove all obvious evidence and two; to help transport the body in relative safety, into the spacious boot of the Skoda. SK drove off silently to their very own RAF-based safehouse and front-line base of operations, in the hope that this clever little precaution would stop them from getting arrested for murder so early into what was going to be a long month.

There was so much still left to do before this nightmare would end, he could ensure the safe return of his girls and calm could descend once again. He suddenly stopped this way of thinking and got on with the task at hand; there were a hundred things which could go wrong if he and SK didn't concentrate.

While SK removed the body, he quietly nipped back into the house and packed a suitcase from Mercer's wardrobe with some warm-weather clothing, his shaving kit, his passport, and the wallet on the table next to the laptop, which Chris also intended to take with him. Considering the amount of time Mercer had spent on it, he assumed he would take it on a vacation no matter how long or short a break it was planned to be. He closed the case and checked the bungalow to make sure it looked tidy. For all intents and purposes, Mercer had gone on holiday. It wouldn't stand up to too much scrutiny, but it would buy some much-needed time. He nudged the laptop mouse, intending to set his e-mail 'out of office' facility to an on-holiday message, again buying time, but the laptop was password protected. It looked like a next-generation security feature was also included, as the alphabetical character box kept dissolving and reappearing. This meant the password changed every 20 seconds, making it impossible to just guess and maybe impossible to crack. Therefore, he couldn't immediately gain access to any programmes, so he stowed the laptop in his shoulder bag, and then exited stage left.

He continued to do everything to avoid detection, so he traversed the very convoluted route back to the allotment shed. He removed his mountain bike from underneath the tarpaulin; it had done a decent job as a stand-in for the motorbike, in profile at least. He had refuelled the motorbike, cleaned the dirt off, let most of the air out of the tyres as it had been that way when he had picked it up, and replaced it exactly as he found it. To all intents and purposes, it had never been out for its midnight spin. He had used the bike because it wouldn't give any secrets away. The motorbike's odometer hadn't been working, which in turn meant the mileage gauge suffered from the same fate. Geoff the neglectful owner would be none the wiser.

He went five rows across to his own allotment shed where he now stowed the bike and his clothes from yesterday. He now stored his night-time stalking gear, along with the now effectively proven, modified rifle and all its constituent parts, safely in a newly secured secret storage compartment, which looked like it was part of the shed back wall. It even had a shelf with empty paint cans secured to it which he had taken the time to build a few days ago so he could come and go with only a small hand-held sports bag. He rested out of sight for a few hours until it was a normal time to be seen out and about. Now in muddy boots and muddy Barbour jacket, he walked to his car which was parked behind the hedge on the allotment side of the fence. He slowly reversed out and then onto lower Long Leys Road and home. No need to sneak about – just a normal guy visiting his allotment. Maybe it was a bit early, it was only 7:15, but allotment owners were known for being a little eccentric.

He had put some tomatoes and carrots in separate bags a couple of days ago to complete the illusion, depending on what time he returned – tomatoes for breakfast and carrots for dinner. Toms today.

As soon as he got home, he plugged the video camera into his laptop, loaded the video into an encrypted file, and viewed it.

It was perfect. It showed Mercer being shot. It showed him falling back like a dead weight, like Pinocchio with his strings cut. It could all be seen even through the ever-decreasing crack in the door, Mercer landing as one big heap on the mat in the hallway. Even in super slow motion and on the highest of high resolution, it was astonishing. You could see the moment of impact and even the look on Mercer's face at the exact moment the lights in his head were turned off. When zoomed to the max, if you looked closely, once the door had quietly shut itself, you could see the automatic bell ringer, which he had only remembered to grab at the very last minute.

He was amazed it had worked so well but this was just the beginning. He hoped the rest of the Kill List would go this well; one down, five to go.

He turned the HDV600 footage into a locked Soft 32 video file which couldn't be altered or tampered with and uploaded it to the e-mail address. He didn't send any message with it, knowing that once MB saw the clip, she would see he was doing as she demanded. Although he knew that letting his family come home was completely out of the question (it was, after all, her only leverage for him completing the job), MB would now have some physical evidence that he had started his task, providing the encryption software was not set to autodelete which he seriously doubted it was, at her end at least.

Nevertheless, he hit the send button and watched it quickly dissolve. The e-mail turned into abstract letters, hieroglyphs and even some randomly generated musical notes, then disappeared into the ether.

Chris was aware he had, in just a single millisecond, given MB more leverage, along with potentially the means of getting him locked away in a high-security prison for the rest of his life. Well, he was going to have to do something about that.

Chapter Twenty-Nine

Lucia heard one of her iPhone alerts. It was playing the first twenty-six bars from the Evita musical composition of *Don't Cry For Me Argentina*. So stirring, so memorable, so like her in many ways, poor little Eva. At last! An e-mail had just arrived. She hoped it would be long-awaited good news.

She climbed down the newly installed loft ladder as she rattled off her instructions. Again, the instructions would definitely be followed to the letter. The example set by B4 had seen to that.

She could see from the phone notification it was indeed good news – an e-mail from Christopher. As she wanted to savour this moment, she went over to her sparse ornate desk, holding only an apple Macintosh next to a genuine desk lamp, circa 1934, the year her father had been born, and a picture of her daughter Catalina. She wanted to be comfortable to enjoy what was to come.

Despite it being only 7:25 a.m., she helped herself to a glass of the 1990 Dom Pérignon, which had been delivered this morning at 6 a.m. from Fortnum & Mason, chilled as requested.

Sitting very comfortably in her high-backed leather chair, she hit the space bar which was all that was necessary to download the message. It turned out to be a video. Well, that came as a welcome surprise; she had felt quite annoyed that she would miss seeing those bastards killed in person, as it were. This was the next best thing. The clever boy had not only given her the chance to see it for herself but had conveniently provided evidence of his wrongdoing. Had he really believed her when she said it would disappear, leaving no trace? Not a clever boy, after all.

She would have Juanita feed and water Sophie and Matilda with real food and water this evening, as a reward, keeping their strength up for the ongoing ordeal. This would have the added advantage of keeping Juanita quiet about their ill-treatment; she never shuts up about it these days.

Sipping her champagne, she just could not help but smile. Her salvation had started in earnest. They do say vengeance is a dish best served cold. Well, this revenge tasted sweet, or was that just the Dom Pérignon?

As she repeatedly watched the video of Mercer being killed, the waves of euphoria rolled over her time and time again and she chuckled to herself. If Juanita could see her, she would think she had gone mad. It had been nearly twenty years since the near toothless old hag had even seen her smile, which was just something she couldn't muster in her presence. Juanita was a constant reminder of so much she had lost, but it was hard for her to extricate the woman from her life. Despite her diminutive stature, she cast a long shadow, the last connection to her once-promising past. For it was she who had helped her bring the only good thing she had ever done into this dark loveless world – her fabulous daughter, Catalina, a gift from the gods. As the saying goes, if the gods want to punish you, they give you exactly what you want, and then take it all away.

The smile slipped from her face just as quickly as it had appeared, leaving only a look of meanness and misery. The memory of her daughter, along with the memory of her beloved father, was the driving force behind everything she did and had done in the past, the present, and the future. She would not stop until vengeance was hers completely. The only way for her to survive was if everyone on her list did not, including Captain Christopher Laser Beem.

Chapter Thirty

Chris sat at his desk, exhausted. It had been quite a few days and they had made some massive leaps forward. He was considering Mercer a success in every way but he was still worried about the fate of his beloved girls. Realising he hadn't eaten for a couple of days, he resolved to rectify this as he would need all his energy for the continuing ordeal. Just at that minute, he heard a ping from his new Yahoo account. It had been set up, obviously by MB, to play a rousing fanfare that Spotify identified as *Himno Nacional Argentino*, which is the Argentine national anthem. The new message warning also needlessly flashed white and light blue horizontal bands – another little message there, only not so subtle this time. This all confirmed that everything was related to the Falklands War, but how and why was still a mystery.

He clicked and read:

Well, about time, LASER.

Family safe, for now. Leave girl on list until last.

Tick tock, tick tock...

El fin de tu mundo.

PS: I am afraid I have been spoiling Sophie and Matilda. They will be getting fat, if I am not careful, so do hurry.

Thirty seconds after it appeared, the message simply shimmied and dissolved; Chris was sure he could hear a small evil-sounding laugh as it did so.

Chapter Thirty-One

SK knew he did not have the luxury of time; it had been spelt out enough times. Being a stickler for detail, he was very aware that it was already down to just less than seven weeks. SK could tell Chris to the minute but knew he didn't need any extra pressure; he knew his friend and mentor would be on the ragged edge as it was. They had decided to divide the tasks to achieve maximum efficiency in the available time left, so SK went to Newark to figure out how best to take the chef, Jerel Jamar (JJ), out of the frying pan and place him firmly in the fire – well, firing line.

Chris went to scope out Mr Builder Man, Dayton, who was working on a new build. He was easy to locate at almost any time of the day. Dayton, it seemed, didn't like to pay rent while he worked, instead ensconcing himself onsite which was convenient for both himself and, as it turned out, Chris.

SK, in the meantime, had booked himself a table at the Blue Oyster Bistro on the Great North Road, an old Roman thoroughfare leading into Newark. It was located just opposite the now derelict twelfth century castle, so he had an excellent view if you liked that sort of thing, which he did. Reading a book about fishing, he was indeed fishing, but his 'catch' was currently in the kitchen filleting a salmon, which was the dish of the day – salmon en croute, crushed new potatoes with minted pea puree, the very food selection SK had made for his lunch. He hoped it was going to be good – he hadn't had a decent meal for a couple of weeks. If this part of the plan was even slightly protracted, he was going to be eating here on a regular basis.

SK had always enjoyed dining out and treated every occasion as an experience. He invariably paid attention to which wine went best with which dish (surprisingly, some reds were better with fish than white). He considered carefully which condiment to use, if any, and then only if it would enhance the delicate flavours the chef had imbued his menu with. He had always thought it was just attention to detail, but it seemed that most of his former wives had thought it was OCD with a little sprinkling of autism. Maybe it was, but was that a bad thing? Not necessarily. Difficult to turn off, maybe, but still, he always made the experience a memorable and enjoyable one.

However, SK's OCD was one of the reasons that their ever-growing files on the Kill List contained the level of detail they did, making the individuals so transparent. Chris was able to pick the exact time and place for the kill shot whilst, most importantly, not getting caught. The only thing that was missing was the why. What linked them together? How did their lives intersect? The answers to these questions remained elusive. Perhaps the laptop from Mercer would shed some light on that.

SK had also reminded Chris that they would need to delegate at least one task if they were simultaneously going to hunt down MB. He still could not get his head around the description Chris had provided for their antagonist. 'Mad-Eye' Moody look alike? He just couldn't visualize it, but from what Chris had said this morning, she was treating Sophie and Matilda well, so that was a bonus. Maybe not so mad after all.

SK had received Chris' blessing to involve an old comrade from their darkest past to help in the search for MB. He had been considering this for a few days, but knew that once he had connected, it would open a whole new can of worms, and there would be no putting that genie back into the bottle. But now he had reached out and set the wheels in motion. He also contacted an old friend of his own, wanting to protect Chris from the legal ramifications of what they were doing. Chris needs to be free to finish his task. He did not like the idea of ending up in prison either, so he was going to do something about that, too.

Chapter Thirty-Two

The file provided by SK was so detailed, so transparent, you would have thought that Chef Jerel Jamar had written it himself.

Chris was able to follow Jamar from the Blue Oyster by taking a parallel route for three miles from Newark to Kelham, arriving only a minute after Jamar at his five-bedroom Victorian Gothic Revival home which he shared with his teacher wife and two teenage girls. SK had staked out the house for three days and had spotted an opening. Chris had spent the last two nights making sure everything was ready so he could execute the plan that night – execute being an unfortunate term, but one he was happy to make happen for the sake of his own girls.

Chris knew from the file that Elizabeth, Jamar's wife, along with Jess and Poppy, went to dance lessons on a Friday without fail. They hadn't missed a class for five years, believing it was important to maintain a routine. It seemed that they did something daily which took them away from the family home for long periods of time; it was almost like they didn't want to be there, despite its grandeur and plenty of open space all around. Well, tonight was no exception. SK reported that Jamar wasn't big on family holidays. However, he had regularly enjoyed golfing breaks with the boys when the mood took him, and it seemed the mood took him on a regular basis.

Chris was amazed at the level of detail SK was able to get; he did engender trust in people. Thank God for that, he thought as he lay on the flat roof of the unused and unloved crumbling children's tree house. It was situated at the south end of what was probably once a beautifully manicured garden but was now left to go wild. 'Six Pines,' it was called. He had only counted five pines, so assumed one had been felled. He was comfortable as he looked through his trusty telescopic sights. He had gotten used to them quicker than he had expected; some things you just couldn't unlearn.

Jamar was sitting in front of his massive computer monitor with his profile to the open window. Open, presumably, to keep the 8Pack OrionX freestanding computer, which SK had noted in the file, cool. That technological beast would need a lot of cooling when it was running at full tilt, and with a price tag of £64,000, you would have thought a fan or aircon might be a good investment. The open window and secluded nature of the rear garden would be perfect for Chris. Additionally, there were no curtains. Jamar clearly wasn't expecting to be spied on. After all, his south-facing garden only had a large shed, five mature pine trees and the old tree house where a fully camouflaged Chris was lying in the prone position. Then it was only open fields all the way to Kelham Hall Country Park. He could not be accidentally seen by anyone.

The chef's 50-inch monitor had a protective security cover which meant you could not see the content of the screen unless you were looking directly at it, face to face as it were. It was the kind of laptop screen which commuters used on trains to stop prying eyes while they fiddled their expenses or someone else's. Maybe Jamar had a secret online business he was keeping from the family, hence, his profile to the door and, in turn, the window.

Jamar in profile was not an issue for Chris, who had worked out that he could shoot him in the right-hand side, fourth rib up. It would achieve the same outcome. The HD video would be harder to achieve from his position on the tree house roof as it had a downward trajectory. To combat the fact that it was night-time, and he would be firing into a room with low-level lighting, Chris had already placed a miniature HD camera on the windowsill so he would be able to get a brilliant 'action' shot for MB. He had also taken the time to attach an ultra-fine clear nylon fly fishing line to the partially open window frame. SK had noted that neither the wife nor the girls went into the back garden, so it was unlikely to be seen. However, he took the precaution of using the pine trees to make sure it was above head height, rendering it invisible to the naked eye. This ultra-thin fishing line would eliminate the chance of him accidentally breaking the window on impact, risking changing the bullet's trajectory even slightly and creating the sound of breaking glass. These were two risks not worth taking. He would need some uninterrupted time to move the body, post-haste, post-shooting.

Jamar had been at his monitor for an hour already, having gone immediately upstairs the second his wife and kids stepped out of the house. Whatever it was must be a thriving side-line, but according to SK, the Blue Oyster menu lacked inspiration, so he wasn't researching recipes.

His mobile vibrated, leaving the screen dark. SK had the Jamar family under observation: all systems go.

Chris was waiting for one natural event to occur, and then he would be good to go. He may be in for a long wait, though, so he rested the rifle butt onto the carry case, never taking his finger off the trigger or his eye from Jamar. This event would be over in a split second. In fact, in the time it took to yawn. Jamar was getting restless, moving from side to side, stretching and rubbing his back. Using the fishing line, Chris had been slowly opening the window at a glacial pace for the last fifteen minutes. Then it suddenly happened. Jamar raised his arms above his head in full stretch and at that moment, Chris fired. Phut. Immediately, with his arms raised above his head like he was surrendering, Jamar dived sideways across the room. Still yawning, mouth wide open, he crumpled against the desk cabinet on his left-hand side, unblinking, dead to this world.

Chris rapidly packed his kit and carefully scaled the well-worn ladder of the once fantastic tree house, rubbing mud on the rungs as he went. While waiting for Jamar, he had been considering whether he could put one up for Tilly, but the thought was too painful, so he had banished it to the recesses of his mind. He dashed across the garden, spooling in the fishing line as he ran. He knew he had plenty of time as Jamar's family were not due back from dance class or the inevitable burger for at least four hours.

He entered the back door via the recently broken (by SK) lock. Another illegal action, this time only breaking and entering. His crimes were mounting up, but he didn't care at this point. He was committed; he was all in. The only thing that mattered was getting Sophie and Tilly back safely, no matter what the cost.

He was far beyond the Rubicon.

Having brought a body bag with him – the sort you see on CSI – he rolled, wiggled, cajoled and coaxed Jamar's body into it, noticing he wasn't wearing trousers. But hell, who cared? He wouldn't need them where he was going.

He let SK know he was ready, then recovered the HD camera and released the nylon line, leaving no indication that anyone except Jamar had been in the room. He easily cleaned up the blood splatter and on leaving, he placed a prepared typed note on the mantle of the living room fireplace. It said, he (Jamar) had gone on a last-minute golf tour with the boys, just arranged this evening. Not as unusual as it sounded, according to SK. And to 'give him some bloody space, woman,' an addition suggested by SK, who, after all, did have considerable experience in this area for better or for worse, called for or not. He also put the contents of Jamar's wallet – a rather large (for a Newark chef, he was no Gordon Ramsay) £979 – under the note, in hope more than expectation that this would buy them the much-needed time to get the job done.

He would like to see what Jamar had been so engrossed in on his computer but when he had fallen, it had triggered an automatic off switch he had been sitting on. Maybe that's why he had been so uncomfortable, and why it hadn't taken very long for him to be in a position for Chris to fire at him. This type of precision shot could take days; he was grateful to the off switch for giving him a chance to flick Jamar's off switch.

Chris, with the help of SK, had carried Jamar's body to the side of this impressive detached house, and alongside the silent Skoda, ready for the trip to Base Waddington.

Once home, Chris again downloaded the HDV600 footage. It was better than he had dared hope for, considering the light and the miniature camera.

You could clearly see Jamar sitting at his computer. You could even make out the movement of his fingers as they travelled across the keyboard like lightning. However, one curious action he hadn't spotted in real-time was that Jamar occasionally stroked the screen. The moment he stretched, it looked like he had dived sideways off his chair, landing in a heap against the cabinet. You could even see the impact of the round as the blood splatter fountained from his right-hand side. It was so quick that his face stayed in full yawn the whole dive. It looked fantastic; Chris was exceptionally pleased with the result. He uploaded the super HD Soft32 video file into the e-mail address and sent it on its way, keeping MB sweet and Sophie and Matilda safe. He would now continue onto the next phase – Bob the fucking Builder.

Chapter Thirty-Three

Lucia was lying on top of her Romantica luxury Italian bed, specially imported and designed to meet her exact specifications. It was identical to the one her father had slept in at the villa they shared when she was just a young girl. His little princess, his only companion. The bed held some incredibly happy memories for her.

The loft conversion had been a labour of love. She had conducted most of the work herself – she didn't want anyone alive to know about this place. Not that Sophie or Matilda would feel that her efforts had been worth it, but if all went well, it would be their final resting place, once her *little project* had been successfully completed.

Her happy ending would only be achieved if Christopher, despite all his efforts, did not get his own happy ending.

She knew he would not – the newly completed loft adaption would make sure of that.

She was just about to head downstairs to the basement's wine cellar to collect a dusty vintage bottle of red for this evening and look in on her guests. She had not seen them for over a week as she did not concern herself with such trivial matters. They were, by just being here, playing their part.

Juanita was allowed to visit them once a day, giving them each two thick slices of multi-seed organic bread, thirty grams of mature Cornish Cheddar cheese, one rustic apple and two litres of London tap water. They would live.

Juanita also emptied the bucket. It had made Lucia smile when she described that aspect to Christopher as 'en suite facilities'. The mental image of comfort it generated was in stark contrast to reality.

As she was passing the 6ft-by-6ft picture of her father hanging in the hall, the alarm on the phone belted out *Evita*. Her heart rate shot up. This could only mean one thing; Christopher had sent her a message. Everything else could wait.

The e-mail came as a surprise. The clever boy had removed all the cameras and the audio device from his home; she could not keep track of his movements so easily these days. B5 and B8 had been losing him daily, and now he was fully operational. Still, what did that matter? As long as he killed those *escoria bastarda pervertida* within the time frame. B1 had reassured her that he was mainly working alone; maybe he had some logistical help. She did not care who helped him if it got the job done. Her busy little B's were there to ensure he didn't come looking for his family, or her, or go to the police. As if he would.

The video of Mr Jamar instantly appeared in glorious high definition. It was a marvel; she was astonished at Christopher's skill. She was doubly impressed with his ability to remain out of police custody. She was sure he would have needed another reminder – maybe a little bit of Matilda in the post – but, no, he was in full action-man mode, which was good for his family but even better for her.

She was actually, despite herself, just a little impressed with the cold-hearted manner with which he was able to murder complete strangers. She knew he had it in him and was more than capable; after all, he had murdered her beloved father.

Chapter Thirty-Four

Beem rose a few days later, now fully rested. After a quick shower, he changed into a suit and tie and headed for lunch at the Wig & Mitre, a local gastro pub and fine dining restaurant. There he had arrange to meet with an acquaintance formally from army intelligence. SK had proven too valuable to fully commit him to locating MB, a task which would require time and a lot of effort. SK had made a recommendation for him to call on an old comrade of his from Intelligence. Chris had agreed wholeheartedly – he needed SK. At Chris' request, SK had briefed Fido who had agreed to meet Chris in person. That was his only commitment, no promises.

Chris knew his house was a no go, having found three micro cameras already and a radio transmitter. He had long suspected they were spying on him, so he wasn't surprised, but his home wasn't an option, and he didn't have time to leave Lincoln. He wasn't 100 per cent convinced this was a good idea, in reality, though he hadn't taken much persuading. SK was right – they couldn't be in three places at once.

So, here he was, against his better judgement. His major concern was the greater exposure which more feet on the ground would generate, creating some unnecessary risk, while his family's fate hung so precariously in the balance.

Fido was one of those military leaders who led from the front. Every soldier wanted to be with him. Even in the fiercest of firefights you just knew he would come through any engagement unscathed, which was how Chris and SK had met him: on active duty, way back in 1979, at the height of the troubles in Belfast. He had been calling himself Elliott Luff and acting as a specialist undercover operative, handling IRA informers for the British.

Chris had been senior operational fire cover for a clandestine recruitment meeting, only for the IRA informer to be an IRA tracker, who was there to remove Elliott from the equation. But first he would want to know all about his current crop of rats, so he had brought a pair of highly trained Rottweilers to pin Elliott down while he did his best to get his information. Only Chris had had other ideas, so mid-maul, he had shot all three – two dead and one in the coccyx, making him a perfect new recruit, a little less able but a lot more willing.

That's how Fido had got his operational nickname.

It seemed that his small collection of friends had, at one time or another, had their lives in his hands, and now so did Chris' family.

He knew Fido could help with the 'why' and the 'who'. He also hoped he would be able to achieve the 'where' as a priority, and if he could convince Fido, he would feel a great sense of relief knowing someone of his calibre had joined the hunt.

He had chosen the Wig & Mitre as it had rooms on many floors. A secluded place with dark, very private little nooks and crannies, nearly every room had sound-reducing wooden cladding, making for a wonderful, intimate dining experience. The layout of the rooms allowed him a chance to have a public meeting which wasn't quite so public.

Chris was enjoying a nice late vintage French Merlot, his first since this nightmare had begun. He felt guilty but it would have looked out of place if he hadn't, so don't judge.

He remembered why he had moved from beer to wine. You try downing a full pint when your surveillance target swallows his small wine in one big gulp, up sticks and leaves. It just drew too much attention. That simple trick had allowed him to remain incognito for many operations. The trade-off was becoming somewhat of a connoisseur. He could now tell you the difference between a Chateau Bovila Malbec or Moret-Nomine just by its distinctive notes.

Chris ordered himself another small wine while he reminisced. One of the benefits of arriving two hours early was that it gave him time to think as well as monitor the various comings and goings. Despite being alone since arrival, he had an unshakable feeling he was being watched, but he just could not see how.

Elliott had been quietly watching Chris in the reflection of the well-polished optics lining the back wall of the lower bar since Chris had arrived. Strategically placed out of sight in the room on the floor above, he hadn't known what to expect, so was here to scope out the place and the man. He trusted SK, with whom he had been in regular contact over the last thirty years, but Chris had just dropped off the radar, so there was no telling what kind of trouble may have come a-knocking. Despite the background from SK, he wanted to look in Laser's eyes – only then would he know the truth. Additionally, it would make a nice change from hiding behind a spreadsheet or staring at a computer screen. Success had proven less fun than he had imagined. A change was as good as a rest, so they say. Well, we'll see, he supposed.

Elliott was not called Elliott and never really had been. He never felt the need to tell anyone his real name; after all, he hadn't used it once in the last thirty-eight years, so today he was going to be Fido once more, anonymity in the familiar.

Chris continued to pretend to sip his red wine when a man in a fedora with long hair flowing from the back of it limped past his table. He was wearing a white shirt with the collar turned up and a long polka-dot scarf with purple glasses.

Chris gave the man a cursory once over and decided he was from the Theatre Royal, situated just down Steep Hill on the edge of town. He resumed pretending to read the menu, keeping an eye on the door, not because he was worried about missing Elliott – ex-military types had a distinctive look – but more in case someone may be observing from team '*El fin de tu mundo*'. Google had translated this to mean 'The end of your world'. He seriously hoped not.

With no sign of any other patrons, he took a little more notice of the menu but was taken aback by the fedora-wearing actor who was now sitting right next to him. He tried not to look too startled but inside, he was all panicked and a trickle of sweat was forming at the base of his neck.

Chris was just about to react when the fedora man held out his hand, saying, "Long time no see, Laser." To his shock and delight, he realized it was Elliott.

"What the hell? Fido, you nearly gave me a heart attack. Why the disguise?" was all Chris could think to say as a form of greeting. "No one knows you here."

He had difficulty believing Fido when he said it was not a disguise, that this was his look. The limp was fake, but the rest was real.

Fido quickly got down to brass tacks, informing him that SK had brought him up to speed with most of the back story, but he wanted Chris to iron out some troubling details.

"I will not get involved unless I'm convinced it's for a good cause," said Fido. "And only if it's the right thing to do. Being an old comrade can only get you so far, Chris," he reiterated.

"Well, at least you're here and that's a good start," said Chris.

"Only because I trust SK," said Fido pointedly.

Chris told Fido, in detail, the full story, starting with his family as hostages and ending with the recent shooting of chef Jamar from MB's Kill List. He also told him the deadline of Thursday, June 14 was a direct link with his past and specifically the Falklands, leaving some important questions; the why, the who, and obviously the where being the key ones.

Fido, despite looking amazed by the shocking story, held up his hands in protest, stating very clearly that he had no intention of going to prison and could never condone murder.

Chris interrupted him, saying, "I haven't finished yet, Fido." He still had the pièce de resistance.

He then explained, in detail, the successful purchase from the gunsmith, and the reengineered L115A3 all-weather sniper rifle, with the additional attachment of an HDV600 video scope.

He explained how they had swapped out the original rifle barrel for a 1:15 deeply grooved with left-hand rifling, 29-inch superlong removable barrel, capable of accurate fire with supreme precision up to 915 feet.

He described, with some pride, how they had adapted a 25 mm calibre peacekeeping 'taser' round, complete with a soft-tipped rubberised bullet which, once encased in its copper shell, produced a powerful electrical charge. This came from the build-up of kinetic energy. Because of its natural spinning motion, it managed to hold enough electrical stopping power to instantly drop a fully grown man or woman, even WWF. The coup de grâce was a blood substitute capsule, containing a solution of blood-red gelatine, gluten, and sugar, giving it the viscosity of blood. It even erupted on impact, giving the splatter pattern which was almost identical to a real lead bullet ripping through major arteries en route to doing some serious internal damage. It had the bonus of being quick and easy to clean up, leaving virtually no trace.

In summary, it renders the victim from the Kill List instantly lifeless. Bloodied, yes! Unconscious, yes! Extremely tasered, yes! Illegal use of food colouring, almost certainly. Dead to the world, but definitely not dead in the real world.

First and foremost, for the safety of Sophie and Tilly, MB would genuinely believe that she had just witnessed, in super high definition, the bloody violent murders she demanded.

Fido simply said, "Fucking aspic!" or perhaps just a few more expletives, deleted. Chris was going to have to get used to how servicemen spoke to each other again and fucking quick.

Fido did add one thing. He knew for certain this would only end for Chris and MB if one, the other, or both were dead.

Chapter Thirty-Five

It was now late in the evening. Chris and Fido had eaten twice at the Wig & Mitre; both meals would have been very enjoyable under different circumstances.

Chris had told Fido about Base Waddington, the location of the bodies – not corpses, warm bodies. SK was fully responsible for keeping them safe, if not over-comfortable, and doing a great job. It was important to find out the link between them. Could they be innocent victims? In his experience, there was no such thing. Plus, MB had gone to too much trouble and expense for that to be true.

Fido liked the plan as it stood: be seen to give MB what she wanted; don't get caught; keep the Kill List alive; find out why they were on the list in the first place; find out their connection; find out why Chris received this task, which could lead to the who, and then the where, freedom for Sophie and Tilly, and end game for MB.

So far, so good. Fido also considered it important to establish why the names on the list were there. He wanted the laptop Chris had removed from Mercer's house. From what Chris had said, it looked like it could be a gateway to connect them all. Jamar and Mercer had both spent most of their free time on their computers. Fido had a tech guru who could help him break the password protection, despite the industrial-level security it possessed.

There were still too many outstanding questions and not nearly enough answers for his liking.

The ever-present 'fly in the ointment' was the police. Eventually, they would get involved. A witness, a family member, a work colleague, or someone from the list, might report them missing. Not an immediate concern but it would lead to an investigation and potentially a more vigilant local police force. Also, it may alert the list, if they were indeed connected, making it impossible to finish the task. That would be the real disaster.

How could they manage the police? And alongside that, the press?

They now had just over six weeks left to keep this all under wraps, which was not going to be an easy task.

Fido had one idea, but it was really out there. A real risk, but only if the person he had in mind said no.

Fido knew one man who could help. You didn't survive, even thrive, in his current business without some high-ranking support for both protection and advice. He often skated on the very edges of the law, so he knew this man could cover both problems.

That man was Freddy 'Three Fingers', which admittedly sounded like the name of an old-fashioned villain from the 1970s TV show *The Sweeney*. In reality, it was one Chief Constable (CC) Charlie Davey who had earned the moniker rather foolishly losing his little finger and thumb on his left hand to frostbite in Norway in 1976. It hadn't stopped him from being a major success in the Marines, becoming something of a hero during the Falklands, and subsequently, on retirement, a highflier in the Metropolitan Police, mainly due to his no-nonsense, can-do attitude. Even now, despite entering the twilight of his career, he was still very hands-on.

Fido travelled down to London to meet with Freddy, who he knew was brave, smart and loyal to a fault, which was why Fido didn't even consider lying to him. It just wasn't necessary. Plus, their mutual trust bank was too easy to overdraw, never to be replenished.

Fido was pleased, even after only a few minutes of small talk and catching up, to see Freddy was still that same person he had known as an officer in the Royal Marines, who held loyalty and service in equal measure. The politics of policing had not erased these qualities. Fido told him everything Chris and SK had been through. Keeping the Kill List alive and safe was the only reason Freddy hadn't immediately sent SCO19 and a specialist tactical firearms team racing up to Lincoln to disarm and detain them. He continued to listen with uninterrupted amazement, and only when Fido had completed his version of the story did he ask Fido to call Chris at once. He wanted to go over it all from the beginning. This had the dual benefit of giving him time to really consider this extraordinary, once in a lifetime request and check the validity of the amazing tale.

Chris was on speaker phone, giving his version of events, leaving nothing out, including the money. Greed wasn't a crime. Actually, it was, according to Freddy.

Freddy couldn't help but be impressed with the moral courage it had taken for Chris to develop a plan which did not involve him in murder. Still, he had broken enough laws for this to be a dangerous request for assistance and strained even his capacity for loyalty. As it was, Chris was going to do jail time. Of that fact he was certain.

He told them both, with no equivocations, that they had really put him in a compromising position. He would have to sacrifice one or the other: comradeship or career. Career lost.

He was only going to assist them while they stayed on this side of murder. He would consider, at a later date, what

163

punishment would be enforced once they had a final tally of the so-called minor crimes. The law was being bent out of shape, but not yet totally broken beyond repair, only on the proviso Chris continued to make every effort to keep this under the radar, as he was managing to do, for now. Freddy was a safety net, not a get-out-of-jail-free card.

Chris agreed instantly. What else could he do? The last thing he needed right now was to get caught.

Freddy hung up on Chris, and at once began to outline his plan of action, firstly to keep this whole sorry mess contained and secondly to catch the real villain of the piece – MB! Or unknown subject 1.

Trying to catch an unsub without any firm background intelligence was both unnerving and unsustainable. It was a situation he was determined would not go on much longer.

Freddy appointed himself as gold commander. His seniority gave him the freedom to manage all the actions and reports pertaining to a crime yet to be reported. He wanted to be one step ahead, if and when that rocket went up. Once that particular circus was in town, everyone would want a piece of him.

He would have to assign some ghost personnel: a DI, faux forensics, constables for imaginary interviews. He would need to fabricate a crime number with a budget, along with a prepared D Notice ready for the press, which would stop news flooding the airwaves, stemming the bloodletting if this ever came out. He couldn't make it last forever; luckily it only needed to last six weeks. Finally, he would prepare a report ready to submit through his chain of command. All this sounded easy, but wasn't, so he was going to need some outside help of his own. He would need at least one 'real' member of his team, someone on the ground, preferably local.

He hadn't overlooked the Kill List. There was not a cat in hell's chance that these people could be innocent of any crimes. His instinct was that it would be best if they remained in custody until they could establish the magnitude of those crimes and what better place right now than Base Waddington? This appealed to his pragmatic and practical nature.

Lastly, he texted Chris, outlining his plan and reminded him, despite the safety net, not to change his modus operandi. It was a distinct style that MB would be looking out for, plus she would still have a few more WWFs for the heavy lifting, you could count on that. He would liaise with Fido going forward.

Chapter Thirty-Six

Freddy sat at his desk, in his massive corner office, room 22.1b, New Scotland Yard, on its highest floor, heading up the Serious Crimes Squad. He was a tired 49-year-old, deeply wrinkled, haggard-looking, bald-headed chief constable. Luckily, his wife of twenty years still loved him because no one else would. He could have taken early retirement on full benefits years ago, a fat gold-plated pension, time served, a job well done, pat on the back, self-evident by the commendations and sets of medals which adorned his walls, but he just couldn't drag himself away from the job he loved and was born to do. He was a villain taker. Whether it was serious organised crime, violent robbery, or sex crimes, these all came under his command. For a reason he could not really put his finger on – maybe it was the hopelessness of it all, the needlessness – his pet hate was sex crimes, in all its guises. They were just so destructive, like a nuclear explosion of hate, affecting everyone and everything they touched. Most victims of sexual abuse physically or mentally never truly recovered. Despite what you may believe, deep down it stays, infecting actions and decisions alike. Buried, maybe, peeking its ugly head out when least expected, but it was always there. These victims needed every ounce of support that he could muster, so he stayed, just to make sure everyone who worked for him did a better job today than they had yesterday. That went for everyone, every day, including him.

He searched 'WATSON', the internal database containing

details of all serving police officers, all levels, and all ranks. It was like a CV vault: who was good at what, where they had served, where they were currently serving, matching skillsets and profiles to operational needs. It was like 'HOLMES', which was the criminal database equivalent, a vault of who's who and who's been a naughty boy or girl and with whom and doing what.

He spent three hours compiling a shortlist of candidates, those he considered he could trust a hundred per cent with this unusual information. Unusual in that, it could get them fired, himself included.

He didn't want to put anyone's career at risk and hoped they would be able to assert enough control to manage the fallout if it came. It was better to plan for the worst and hope for the best.

His top candidate had some real advantages in that she knew him very well and was local, currently stationed at Lincolnshire Police Headquarters.

Detective Chief Constable (DCC) Nicky Brown (also known as Nicky Nails) had graduated from Hendon College the same year as Freddy. Although ten years younger, she was still his peer and they had also been on some successful serious criminal operations together when cross-division support was required or requested.

Nicky had been one of those officers who naturally stood out, not trying to impress anyone, just determined to do the job and do it well. She had been offered a fast track to promotion, but she had politely declined in favour of earning her stripes, as it were the rank-and-file route. She had earned her place in the higher echelons of the force, along with the respect of all her subordinates, engendering trust and esprit de corps along the way. She had also earned the nickname 'Nicky Nails' – hard as nails, not the polished type – but no one would dare to call her that to her face. Despite her long flowing golden hair and angelic features, she was no angel. If you set a low standard, which you then failed to maintain, she would kick you up the arse. She set a high standard, which she never failed to maintain.

Freddy called her PA and set up a meeting in his corner office; there were no more secure locations in the Yard.

Nicky arrived twenty minutes early, as was normal for her, from Riseholme Divisional Headquarters, on the outskirts of Lincoln.

Freddy greeted her with his usual bearhug, reserved for only a handful of trusted individuals. Coffee and small talk were over before the aroma had cleared the room. He felt it would be best to ask Nicky to listen to the complete story before asking any of the many questions she would have, so he began.

Freddy first lightly tested the water with two questions to confirm what he thought he already knew:

1. The role of AC-12 in policing and what it really meant?

2. How far would she be prepared to go, to achieve the outcome over procedure?

Nicky was sure the AC-12 often investigated the wrong coppers, finding fault where there was only a genuine desire to 'do the right thing'. She understood simply bending some rules which, by design, hogtied and hitched officers. Removing these restraints often led to important villains being taken off the street, but liberal lobby groups were doing their utmost to constrain real officers. In the real world, villains didn't have such constraints, so nor should real detectives.

Question one – Ouch. **Pass**.

Nicky said despite the glaring contradiction between being seen to do everything by the book, it was clearly rewritten just to cope with an oversensitive oppressive politically correct governing body which led to unsound arrests of petty non-crimes disguised as hate crimes, while drug kingpins, rapists and people smugglers walk free.

Freddy stopped Nicky there and calmed her down. He knew hundreds of frontline officers of all ranks who shared the same sentiments.

Question two – So true. **Pass.**

Freddy then told Nicky everything, from soup to nuts, leaving nothing out in between.

Nicky was astounded. Declining Freddy's offer to immediately leave and not look back, the outstanding questions were just too tantalising for her. There was something important going on here, no doubt, and she wanted to know what that was. Freddy couldn't tell her who MB was. Or how Chris managed to make an electrical base sniper rifle. A long-range stun gun would come in very handy when this was all over, she smiled. The Kill List – there had to be more to that than met the eye. It looked like someone was cleaning the house. But whose house and why?

There must be loyal highly paid soldiers helping the Mad Bitch. WWF was a Bosnian drug dealer – there was a clue there. A lot of muscle became suddenly available when the Bosnian-Serb War ended in 1995. Finally, who had come up with those ridiculous names? This time she laughed out loud when Freddy wiggled the remaining digits on his left hand.

Accepting they were working in the dark and on faith, not reassured but fully committed, Nicky would trust Freddy's judgement on this. He had just as much to lose. She would do everything in her considerable powers to help Freddy and, in turn, Chris and his ever-growing team.

Chapter Thirty-Seven

Chris awoke from a nightmare-inducing dream, into a nightmare-inducing reality. He lay on top of his bed, familiarising himself with his surroundings, and feeling disorientated. The dream was always the same: he had managed to defeat MB, but even with all the help of the new team, he never ever found his beautiful girls. In the dream, he continued to search until he was an incredibly old man. It felt like he was free-falling directly into Hades; the search was continual within Dante's nine concentric circles of hell. It felt like that when he was awake most days now. He remembered a time when it hadn't been like this. It was painful to relive, but he needed a timely injection of moral courage for the tasks at hand, so he let the memories flow with more clarity.

He settled on a strong memory from just twelve months ago. A family camping holiday in the Lake District near Windermere where Tilly loved to sail. They had taken two tents but had spent the whole week with all three sleeping in one, so comfortable were they in each other's company and within themselves. It just seemed so natural.

Fishing, sailing, hiking, and cooking on an open fire, seeing who could make the other laugh the most – it had been Tilly, for the most part. They had laughed so hard for most of the week, by the time they arrived back home, it felt like they'd had plastic surgery; their face and stomach muscles were so tight through their whole bodies shaking with natural laughter.

A warm salty tear rolled slowly down Chris' cheek, prompting him to get on with the rest of the Kill List. But first, he wanted to debrief SK and get his latest file notes. He also wanted to bring him up to speed on the developments from Fido and Freddy, which were significant. What better place to do this than Base Waddington?

Mercer and Jamar were no worse for their extreme tasering or by being drugged and dragged into a form of protective custody.

SK had surpassed himself, dressing the pair of captives in such a way that once this was all over, they could be released, unharmed from whence they came. They would not be able to identify their captors, not even by voice recognition.

He gave the captives warm tea in plastic cups with straws protruding from the lids, like toddlers' sippy cups, so they could drink without having to remove the one-piece rubber S&M gimp suits which now covered them both from head to toe. The zip at the mouth let them breathe and eat, a simple painless control mechanism. Chris would have dearly loved to watch SK getting them into these costumes; it must have been a hilarious spectacle. Currently lying on the recently acquired mattresses (actually recovered from a house fire near Boston along with some navy army blankets), a makeshift bathroom could be used whilst shackled to the wall, using the anal zips for exit only; God bless the S&M community. It was a comical but practical sight.

Chris had never intended to kill anyone, despite evidence to the contrary. As long as his girls remained safe, so would everyone else. Except, maybe, MB.

SK had dropped a bombshell on Chris' arrival at Base Waddington. It seemed Dayton had gone skiing in the Alps, specifically Chamonix so he could ski Mont-Blanc. He would be gone for ten days at least – oh, the life of a single man – so they had selected a new target. They both agreed it would be prudent to abduct the only other single man on the list; he was less likely to have an army of close family knocking on the police's door. The four remaining empty beds were a reminder of the Herculean nature of the task still ahead.

This candidate was going to be an interesting challenge, more morally than physically.

The Reverend Dr Noah William Morris-Hargreaves, the Subdean of the Lincolnshire Dioceses, would not be easy to abduct. He was constantly on the move, visiting the local archdiocese, attending Sunday schools, normal schools, prayer meetings, and the youth pastors' outreach programme, all the while teaching the doctrine of the church, conducting the sacrament twice daily and three times on Sundays. He was very rarely alone, and always locked away in medieval buildings, performing medieval practices.

Not being a devout man himself, Chris didn't understand the reverence these men commanded, especially in the light of the ongoing controversies surrounding the Catholic Church's sexual abuse cases, still persisting to this day. It wasn't all-pervasive but it turned his stomach to even think about it.

He would treat this one the same as the rest. He had too much at stake to worry about hurt feelings or a few bumps and bruises. The Rev lived in a remote part of the bishop's lodgings which was within easy walking distance of the eleventh century cathedral. It was nicely tucked away within its own grounds, behind a twelve foot high circular stone wall which surrounded the lush hibiscus border with deep shrubbery within its well-manicured garden.

He had retrieved his ghillie after his own eyes-on recce

conducted earlier in the afternoon, then had settled himself and his modified rifle into a position affording a view directly in the room with a piano, presumably the music room. He had selected this vantage point while reviewing the reconnaissance pictures and the hand-drawn layout provided by the ever-active SK. (He had managed to produce these while cleaning the windows of a nearby top flat which he, himself, had dirtied with mud from the roof, and so had cleaned them for free!)

The twelve foot high walls gave the Rev a sense of security he really shouldn't have had. It had only taken a further two motionless nights until Chris had a clear shot directly through the open sash window, with the video running. Chris took his time and on the third night, the breeze had picked up a little and was in the right direction. This prompted the Rev to slowly walk to the window which Chris had opened two nights ago. On reaching it, he raised both his frail-looking, naked arms to slide it shut. That was the exact action Chris had been waiting for – his opportunity was here. A quick look around, control breathing, slowly exhale, hold, hold. Phut! Instantly, the round exploded at the sweet spot, the electrical charge knocking the Rev clean out and backwards onto the music room rug, the blood splatter a perfect heart shape. Dead as a dodo. Well, out like a light. One more for Base Waddington.

He quickly disassembled the rifle, unscrewed the suppressor, and loaded the parts into the gun case. He added the ghillie suit, shouldered the lot, and called SK, who was parked just along the road, on the walkie-talkie. Skirting around to the rear entrance, Chris dashed into the music room. The Rev's careless sense of security meant the outside door was unlocked. Chris found him, as expected, still out cold. This wouldn't last long so he quickly sedated him with a small amount of ketamine, which SK had bought for cash, along with six sets of bondage gear, at a drive-through sex shop along the A1 just past Newark. No questions asked, even the quantity hadn't raised an eyebrow.

Rolling the Rev up in the music room rug contained the faux blood. His heart leapt when he noticed the laptop was still up and running. The old perv was looking at a porn site; he thought perhaps the Rev was going to enjoy the bondage part of his ordeal after all.

Mindful that if he closed the laptop lid its security would be triggered, he was also aware that it would auto shut down if he didn't tell it to stay awake. He removed it carefully with its charger. As he opened the front door, he buzzed the electronic gates.

SK glided through, parked with the rear of the van by the door so they could load the rolled-up Rev, the gun case, the food bag and the poo bag – when you've got to go, you've got to go. Chris quickly tidied up and left a scrawled, spidery note: 'Travelling to York Minster for an ecclesiastical conference on emergency relief.' Any housekeeper would wait a day or two before challenging the note.

Chapter Thirty-Eight

The priority for DCC Nicky Brown right now was the 'who' and 'why these particular people on this particular Kill List?'

My God! Was she really condoning supporting someone who was working his way thought a Kill List, even if his special brand of murder was better than the alternative – actual murder?

These priorities would only change if the abductions became common knowledge, or if Chris got caught. They would change dramatically if he actually killed someone, even by mistake. That wasn't acceptable or part of the plan.

Perhaps Fido or SK would be able to help, so while she was still in London, prior to returning to Lincoln tomorrow, she asked to meet them later. SK was in London to meet Fido and it turned out they were dining at The Ivy that evening and asked her to join them. She wondered how she would explain the dinner on her monthly expense report, so decided not to even try.

Mindful of how sensitive the whole operation was, no police activity would be as bad as too much around the cleverly crafted deception Chris was so remarkably still pulling off. It could arouse the suspicion of MB, leading her to execute (poor choice of words) her much-promised reprisal on his family without delay. It was a fine line they were tiptoeing down. There was not only the family to protect, but the innocent bystanders – so-called collateral damage – and their own skin to worry about. Failure at any point would mean she and Freddy would both be out of the job, by virtue of the fact that they would both be in some high-security prison. Nicky was a natural worrier, it actually helped her keep ahead of the disaster curve, but this was a new level, even for her.

There was a mountain of faux paperwork, faux files, faux operational reports, some faux forensics, and even some faux red tape on top of faux red tape, which gave them the ability to brief the Deputy Assistant Commissioner if it became necessary. Unless some human bodily waste matter and a large industrial fan collided, they had at least got some control of the police side of this challenge of challenges.

Nicky could now concentrate on the list. She had to stop calling it the Kill List. It unnerved her too much; it seemed too macabre.

The list proved to be an enigma, wrapped up in a puzzle, inside an electronic conundrum. Nobody on the list had a record (not even speeding), no juvenile record expunged or sealed, as far as she could tell, nothing in HOLMES, nothing in the local or national newspapers, no acts of value, nothing of merit whatsoever. They also did not have a social media presence. They were ghosts, leaving no footprint either digitally or physically. That alone was a massive red flag and pointed a guilty finger at them all. A list of people who seemed to have nothing in common, ethnicity, age, or gender, who, by association, were guilty of one thing only – not being guilty of anything. There it was, your common denominator, which now became the only known fact about the list, apart from the fact that two-thirds were temporarily residing at Base Waddington. She imagined they would, by the fullness of time, be grateful for that fact – the alternative was not going to make them feel any better. She didn't suppose anybody whose name appeared on a Kill List ever really got over that fact, innocent or otherwise.

That evening she would learn two more facts. One, Fido was none the wiser about why the list had been compiled and two, Sketchley was surprisingly good company.

She, like the rest of the team, did not enjoy working in the dark.

Little did they know that was all going to change dramatically now that SK had the holy grail, for this mission at least – an active [awake] laptop plugged into a portable power supply, which he had taken down to London earlier that day for Fido to forensically examine. Let there be light. The laptop held heavily encrypted files and website URLs which they would have had no hope of cracking in the time available. As it was, it could still take weeks, which was time they did not have.

Fido had already been trying to crack Mercer's laptop with no success due to the industrial level of security, which was a match for him and his team. Now, having the Rev's laptop alive and kicking, as it were, would hopefully prove more obliging.

Chris loaded the Rev's ultra-high-resolution encrypted file to *lapampas@job.com.ar.* It wasn't quite as good as the previous one – the curtain had masked the look on the Rev's face – but you could clearly see he was no longer part of this world. This was true up to a point, as he was now part of SK's S&M world of wonder.

Three down, three to go. Now he concentrated on Dayton who was back from skiing in two days. He would also be the next least bad option.

He knew from the ever-growing file that Dayton was starting a new build at the far end of the Brayford Pool, next to the Hilton Hotel, a beautiful part of the city with waterside residences, great restaurants and some lovely waterside pubs. The new building site would cause a few problems but would provide many more opportunities if you knew how to exploit them. SK had studied the layout, the comings and the goings on and off the site. Now, to his good fortune, he had seen a spot which was almost a purpose-built observation post. Fortune favoured the brave.

Ping... No fanfare playing this time.

Your girls remain as safe as they ever were, whilst enjoying the same level of comfort.

I am sure you have figured it out by now; your past has finally caught up with you, not before time.

Why is the deadline so important to me, and by association important to you? Can you remember what you were doing on Monday, June 14, 1982 at precisely 11:55 a.m. on the Malvinas?

Well, I do, you murdering bastardo!

Remember, leave the girl until last or I will kill one of your girls.

El fin de tu mundo.

The curtness of the e-mail, the occasional Spanish expletives, and the exact time reference, told him everything he needed to know. MB was the General's daughter.

Chapter Thirty-Nine

Fido's day was getting better and better. Firstly, he had found an IP address embedded in the e-mail code which was allowing MB to secretly communicate with Chris and vice versa. He had made several attempts to get through the firewall, but it would take more time than he thought he had available, so he settled down to probe the open 'live' laptop from the Rev.

The Rev's lack of technical awareness had let them into the underlying computer code where they found sets of encryption keys. Fido then was able to deploy an algorithm to unscramble all the hard drive messages. Normally, they would be hidden on a remote server, but the Rev hadn't cleaned up his data for months, maybe years, and there it all was.

Links to private chat rooms, a pay-per-view secure video vault, secure closed-link group meeting rooms, dark web URLs to sex sites, incognito search options, porn websites, everything. Lady luck was really on their side now, because if he had linked to any file, site, or message contained on this computer, it would have completely destroyed the hard drive through a highly sophisticated application called 'Forrest' fire security. It would wipe the memory completely and all data would have been unrecoverable, turning the laptop into a very expensive paperweight. This was very, very sophisticated and highly technical stuff, but in the hands of the Rev, it was wasted. He hadn't set the Firestarter hotkey, which meant his laptop stayed awake permanently instead of automatically shutting down after three seconds unless pressure was applied to any key, or as in the case of Jamar, a security pad to sit on. The Rev's technological ignorance was the team's salvation. Praise be to God.

It did not take Fido long to realise why there was a James Bond-level of security. All the names on the list were in one private group meeting room of super users who all shared an unhealthy obsession with one specific topic – explicit, detailed, underage sex. There were 30,000+ hours of full-length videos in the vault; all young, innocent-looking victims of bondage, torture, mutilations, and multiple rapes.

Fido only had the stomach for twenty minutes and that was enough. There were 500,000+ images of girls, boys, and even toddlers. Fido guessed between three years to fifteen years old, no more. He didn't have the willpower to study them for longer. There were 'live' video links, including a countdown clock to when the site became active. There was an event history archive, available for the previous video feeds; you could rent or buy any of the videos. They went up in price as the ages came down.

The group were a little cavalier with the distribution of this disgusting filth; never in their wildest dreams had they considered they would be caught. They had clearly paid vast sums of money for the highest level of security. The Rev was paying £10,000 per month for unlimited access. It had kept them secure to live their fantasies and perversions for decades, only for the Rev to be caught with his pants down, literally.

Fido's hands were now shaking. You just could not unsee these appalling images. He looked down at the dossiers SK had created around the so-called Kill List. This whole list had just become so much more important; it was now a list of a previously unknown paedophile group. The collective noun must be a danger of paedophiles.

One thing which did occur to him was that whoever had put this list together had surely known the sexual proclivities of the group. It was impossible to link them in any other way, so why hadn't MB just reported them to the authorities? Or was this all part of her little fantasy, making Chris do her dirty work before killing him herself? Either way, the names and pictures on the list took on a much more sinister and threatening tone now. Their evil seemed to be creating its own smell, a stench which Fido was having trouble keeping under control. He had, like most people, heard of paedophiles, but never had he imagined he would come within touching distance of a single one, let alone a whole bloody group of them.

The impact on Fido was palpable. His hands were still shaking when he phoned Freddy, and they still were when he phoned SK. He set up a meeting, with no excuses, no delays. This shit had just become very real, very fast, for all parties.

They had to be exceptionally careful; it was too important to fuck this up. Their A+ game was needed. They must put this sick motherfucking paedophile group out of commission once and for all, and directly into the hardest fucking jails in the land. Obviously, when Fido was stressed, he reverted to type and right now he was fucking stressed.

He then threw up into the wastepaper basket next to his desk. It was a pity it was a wicker one with no bag – he would clean that up later.

Chapter Forty

Their collective shock was palpable. Everyone in the room was speaking at once and it became a crescendo of noise. Chris banged his hand on the table, trying to get some order. He still had a task to do and was on the clock.

So dumbfounded and numb with shock, the disgust had swelled so quickly, that it had the feel of a tropical storm or a hurricane, dragging along a cyclone of revulsion and rage. They all wanted vengeance for the victims and for their families. Like Fido, none of them had ever believed they would come this close to this level of depravity. It was the sort of thing you read about in the newspaper or saw in a film. Everyone on the list had looked so normal, so next-door neighbourly. No one – no one – would have guessed their wicked depraved connection.

It was transparently clear that this team alone held the absolute power to expose this ring. They were now the embodiment of the scales of justice, able to bring the full weight of the law down on these bastards.

Fido had shown them images, videos, names and data, leaving them in no doubt this was just the tip of a very big iceberg. It seemed that Jamar was not only filming the sick depraved acts but selling them online worldwide, making millions in the process. But where there was pay-per-view, there would be payment records. Payment records meant bank accounts or credit cards, which meant personal data – hard evidence. It would take a lot more time and resources than the team could muster. They knew that currently, they would make only a very small dint, but they were definitely going to stop this Lincoln-based ring.

Freddy, Nicky and Fido had promised once this current operation 'save family' was concluded, they would continue to identify every person found on the laptop or in any of the pay-per-view vaults. This would become their top priority, their life's work. They must curtail the distribution completely, as a starting point. The one burning question bothering them all was how had MB known about this paedo ring?

Was she a participant or victim?

Freddy quickly took the lead. Again, everyone was grateful they had involved the police, stopping things from getting out of control. He needed to make sure they were all in step and acted as one body; no taking justice into their own hands, no lynch mobs, despite the warm feeling which that concept produced in him when he imagined them all swinging from a rope. It was a pity that capital punishment couldn't be reinstated, for paedophiles at least. In his book, this was worse than any other type of crime, except maybe first-degree murder, just!

He wanted Chris to step up his timeline. It was clear that everyone on the list had an intimate connection and would soon be alerted to the absentees, maybe alerting every person in the database, maybe sending them all to the ground. Then how could Chris complete MB's task? How would he be able to keep his family safe? This was still the main priority for all in attendance.

Freddy and Nicky had put their police inspectors' hats back on and were keen to start, what they considered would be, going back to the day job. To bring this ring and everyone associated with it to book, they would need to involve wider global task forces – FBI and Interpol – soon, to help lock up the dirty little lot of them. Nicky had been sure this list was key but never had she thought it would turn out to be this important.

The irony was that MB had sent one man who was a proven killer to kill her Kill List to save one family, only for him to end up saving all the victims, all the families, and all the list, ultimately saving his own life in the process. The fact that the only killer was MB herself, the General's daughter, was not lost on Nicky.

The challenge was obvious – how to protect their next victim, save the Beem family, find, capture, and charge MB with murder, and still be able to press charges against the complete list for their monstrous crimes... That was all!

Chapter Forty-One

Chris and SK left the meeting under the cover of darkness via a convoluted route, some two hours prior to the rest of the group disbanding. They were, as always, careful to make sure not to be caught, in the eleventh hour, by MB's Bosnian war veterans.

He dropped SK off quickly and collected his gear from the allotment shed. He was in no mood for any drama. His mind had been preoccupied with thoughts of what MB might do to Sophie and Tilly. He had, after all, shot and killed her father, the General, despite it being in defence of the realm and the people of the Falkland Islands, as part of his job as the task force's main sniper. It didn't matter to MB that it was a legitimate act during an illegal war. She had been harbouring a grudge for nearly thirty years and she was fixated on him and her Kill List of paedophiles. No doubt, she hoped he would be caught, tearing him away from his family forever, and effectively ending his once-happy life as assuredly as if she had killed him herself.

He now also wanted to make sure he completed the full list, getting these scum off the streets as soon as possible. But the further he got, the more likely it was possible that there would be a witness, which may even play into his hands with MB getting some genuine news coverage for a change. Freddy and Nicky would have to field the inevitable fallout which came with it. They had promised they could. He had given them notice, and now he was going to put that particular promise to the test.

He parked in the underground car park between One The

Brayford, a smart new hotel, and the Hilton Hotel, which was opposite the FossWay Commercial building site.

SK had been down to see Gunny overnight and had collected another batch of the highly modified rounds, along with an additional weapon which Chris had designed for close quarters – a handheld pistol. It was similarly capable of firing slightly smaller taser rounds, still an electronic round, complete with a synthetic blood capsule, effective only at short range. He was wearing a high-definition helmet camera fitted onto his cycle hat, allowing him to share the footage with MB, aka Lucia, as they had found out yesterday.

He had learnt that Lucia had been in the Falklands at the time he had removed the General from his command of the invading forces, permanently.

What came afterwards was pieced together through statements from prisoners-of-war and reports of war crimes. Evidently, Lucia had been beaten and raped by the feared elite 601 Intelligence Battalion death squad commanders as an act of retaliation for the loss of their turf war and the humiliating defeat. Her whereabouts after the conflict were unknown. She had simply disappeared completely, rumoured to be living off her father's plundered millions back in South America.

He couldn't understand why she would hold it all against him personally; he was just performing the duties assigned to him. He was one of the thousands of men battling to regain control of British sovereignty. Knowing he couldn't change her perception of events, he got on with the task at hand, staying in the dark recesses of the building site's second-floor entrance, where he could see most of the comings and goings without much chance of being seen himself. Dayton parked his Range Rover on the opposite side of the road on double yellows. Chris knew he would have to move the vehicle quickly, or he would bring about unwelcome attention.

As Dayton climbed the stairs, his face was contorted with some intractable problem or other. Chris could only guess at what was on Dayton's mind and hoped it wasn't the fact that Chris had most of his paedophile-ring buddies in cages at old RAF Waddington. That might put him on high alert and Chris needed a clean shot. There would be no second chance. Luckily, Dayton was too distracted to notice Chris as he knelt calmly, arms extended in front of him, aiming chest height, just a few paces in from the second-floor entrance. When he finally did notice Chris, it was too late. BANG!

Bannnnng bannnng bannnng bannng banng bang.

Jesus, the fucking echo rang throughout the entire empty building site. It seemed to go on forever. Gunny had not been able to make a muzzle suppressor in the time available. *Time to move the Range Rover now,* he thought. He had to move fast before he become an internet sensation, so he swiftly gathered up his kit and dragged Dayton to the rubbish shoot. He promptly dropped him down, feet first, onto the pile of old dirty blankets, a couple of mattresses and some old stinking clothes Chris had gathered together from different floors, left behind by rough sleeping local tramps. He hoped any damage to Dayton's lower regions wouldn't be too serious. He had, after all, promised Nicky, but he also hoped it would hurt like hell when the bastard came to. Bundling Dayton into the Range Rover was relatively straightforward, but he could, however, hear the sirens wailing in the distance. The gunshot had obviously been reported to the police and, in turn, the press. Win-win.

He was very pleased to be away from prying eyes, and even more importantly, prying iPhones, denying them the new trend of making YouTube clips or selling them to the press. That would be hard to explain to Freddy who would be extremely pissed off. No one could have predicted this turn of events, not even Nostradamus. Chris let Fido know Dayton was in the bag, literally.

Once at Base Waddington, the only difficult part was the change of Dayton's clothes from his builder's kit to the S&M onesie, as it was a little too small. It was going to be extremely uncomfortable until their eventual handover to Freddy. Another win-win, then.

Freddy had received ten phone calls, including three frantic ones from Nicky, along with twenty-five e-mails about the sound of shooting. Once Fido confirmed that Chris had got clean away, Freddy set about amending his reports, calming down Nicky and generally making up details to be included in the latest up-to-the-minute developments in the operation. He added some minor details for the case to remain realistic and collated all the reports. He stood down as a diligent 'real-life' duty officer and conducted, via the phone, a fictional handover to his ghost officers. He initiated a Skype press briefing, complete with a press pack which included pictures of the massive blood splatter pattern, and some .357 Magnum shell casings, to explain the loud gunshot in his faux report. The shells were actually from an old 'solved' murder case from thirteen years ago in North London. There would be no chance of any real evidence contaminating the faux crime scene, or getting in the way of the general assumptions in circulation. These assumptions now included the suspicious disappearance of Nathan Dayton – currently revered local building king, soon to be reviled local building pervert bastard. He had a lot of jail time coming, to enjoy in the company of 'scum-of-the-earth' types who would very quickly know all the paedophile's home truths and no doubt hammer a few home truths of their own into Dayton. So, a lot of pain coming his way. Another win-win, then.

Nicky, following Freddy's lead, had briefed the local CC and then the local press who ate it up with a spoon. Lincolnshire had always been very short on murder, kidnappings or any other major crimes. Stolen bikes they had in spades, but potential killings, no. So, this was a press field day, and whilst they wanted to make hay while the sun was shining on their little piece of turf, they were thwarted at every turn, and in the end, only had the press pack to resort to. None of the usual suspects could shed any light, no inside source could be quoted, and no leaked case files were shared in a 'breaking story' exclusive. There was no money changing hands, under the table or over the counter. Nada, nought, zilch, zero. It didn't stop them from making up some gory details, of course, which was all good for the narrative. Free publicity was grist to the mill and fed MB's twisted idea of retribution, so that helped.

Their lives and their actions were serious now. They all knew the stakes were high, as high as they were ever going to be. One slip could mean ruin for them all. More importantly, the paedo ring would be free to practise their depravity unchallenged, not to mention the fates of Sophie and Matilda, if they got any part of this wrong.

Chapter Forty-Two

Lucia was having a genuinely pleasant day, for once. She had just returned from Harrods where she had lunched on smoked salmon, quails' eggs, and truffle shavings, and enjoyed a particularly nice early vintage 1998 Dom Pérignon brut champagne. She allowed herself a brief little smile. It was not just the champagne that was making her mood light, it was also the latest video from Christopher. The clever boy had actually shot the bastard, Mr Dayton, at close range, something she had envisaged. She had supplied the Bersa for that purpose, but seeing it so up close and personal was something that gave her an immense feeling of satisfaction. It was the look of genuine shock and sheer terror in his depraved little piggy eyes. Now that was a pleasure to behold; a real pleasure, to be savoured like this Dom.

If Christopher had been one of her little B's, she would have rewarded him with a million dollars. Instead, she would let his girls enjoy some light this evening and even let Juanita feed them real food, unrestrained. Yes, today everyone was having a good day, except Dayton, admittedly, who Lucia knew was now rotting in hell along with the other child killers. Her. Child. Killers.

Ahhh! Now her deep dark mood was creeping back. It always did at the smallest of thoughts or slightest mention of Catalina. Her default setting had been of hate and bile for so long now that she could no longer control it.

Lucia could feel herself slipping back into a haze of self-induced recriminations, sinking in the quicksand of deep despair. The closer the end date came, the deeper she went, and the more unrelenting her spiral into oblivion became. It cast her around, flinging her into abject blackness which absorbed her whole until there was nothing left of Lucia. Only evil and loathing.

The video she had watched on a loop for twenty minutes had not given her the relief she had prayed for. It was therapeutic in its own way, but like any drug, she craved more, more frequently. She had taken to tormenting Sophie and Matilda, but even that had lost its appeal. Beating Juanita had not even raised her pulse.

She had killed B7 for falling down on his job and leaving her vulnerable to a cyber-attack. Two hackers had tried to get through her firewall and software security. The computer was buzzing with activity. Still, it would not matter. It would soon be over, just like Vedad, commonly known as B7.

In hindsight, it was actually a good idea to give Christopher a little helping hand. The firewall she had in place was impossible to crack and she would want him here eventually. Maybe B2, aka Vildana, would prove useful in this regard.

She satisfied herself in the knowledge that the paedophile scum-of-the-earth on her list, who had raped, tortured, and killed her beautiful daughter Catalina, would all be dead, dead, dead, DEAD!

Sophie would be dead, dead, dead, DEAD! Why should he have beauty?

Matilda would be dead, dead, dead, DEAD! Why should he have hope?

The man who had, by his actions, started this whole living nightmare by killing her beloved father – her God, her General – Captain Christopher Laser Beem, would be dead, dead, dead, FUCKING DEAD! Why should he have life?

All this screamed in her head, making her dizzy.

Chapter Forty-Three

Surprisingly, there was no message from MB, although he was sure she had received the headcam video of Dayton. It looked so real, that it appeared to be filmed by Alfred Hitchcock himself. The shadows enhanced the look of terror on Dayton's face at the moment the ear-splitting gunshot echoed around the building site. It looked like he was in one of those computer games – MB would be able to see the flash from the muzzle of the pistol and she would see the impact mark as Dayton was hit one inch left of his heart. She would see him dropping to his knees, then slowly keeling forward. Then fade to black.

Chris and SK were sitting in the Skoda reviewing the last thirty minutes of their joint operation and wondering if the phrase *'the best-laid schemes o' mice an' men'* had ever been as fitting as right now.

Chris had been staking out Ryvita House, the name locals called the building of their city police station, due to the stone cladding adorning the outer walls. He was ready to follow Inspector Raby for what they hoped would be the last time. Once Raby had parked his car in the multi-storey directly opposite his flat and vacated the vehicle, Chris planned to 'shoot' him there. Helpfully, he had put a reserved plaque (illegally) in bay twenty-nine, right next to the stairs on the second floor. It was a nice dark corner with no prospect of prying eyes – important at this last stage in the operation.

Raby was a creature of habit, a man who clearly liked a

normal routine, which seemed unusual for someone with his sexually depraved, despicable desires.

Raby followed his usual route, as witnessed for the last week by SK and the last two days by Chris, who had set himself up ready for the 'kill shot'. The video camera was set up and he was virtually undetectable to the untrained eye, being underneath a Range Rover that he had immobilised earlier this evening, prior to SK following Raby from the police station. So far, so good.

Chris lay motionless for two hours behind a black cotton mesh running the length of the Range Rover's underside, aiding in the concealment. He checked his watch just once to confirm Raby was now overdue by eleven minutes. Unusual, but not a disaster. Several minutes later, he received a call on his Whispernet headset earpiece. The only sound it made was in his ear; no one would overhear anything. He quickly pressed his throat mic intercom, one click and release. SK would know he was listening, so he listened. Shit, shit, and double shit.

Raby had been arrested en route home. Holy fucking shit!

He was finding it difficult to remain calm. What would this do to MB? Would she see it as a betrayal, a failure of his making? If so, would she take it out on Sophie or Tilly? That thought scared him more than he would ever admit. He composed himself long enough to carefully and swiftly pack up his rifle, along with the rest of his kit, including the HD camera. Once on the first floor, and looking like any other person travelling home after a long hard day, he didn't have to try awfully hard to look haggard. He had, after all, been running ragged for the last two months, all for one goal – to save the ones he loves. Now it seemed he had failed at that.

SK picked him up and drove him to the rear entrance of the Lincolnshire showground because it had no traffic cameras or

CCTV. It was only a mile out of town but had a 360 panoramic view, so they would not be followed or tracked. SK had double-checked the vehicle this morning – no bugs, no trackers, even the vehicle's GPS had been disabled as an extra precaution, extra insurance.

SK smiled, and simply said, "Here, mate!" then innocently placed a cardboard box on his lap. Chris smiled for the first time that night. SK had presented him with a full colour, whisper clear audio, HD video of Raby's arrest – all blue lights, sirens, all guns blazing arrest – on the outer circle, a public ring road, in full public glare, full press spotlight, the full nine yards. This would go a long way towards placating MB, giving Chris time to set up the final spectacular action, within the deadline. He knew it would be the only way he could stop MB from killing his girls. She didn't make idle promises.

Once at Base Waddington, Chris sent the masterstroke which was SK's video of Raby's arrest, along with the hastily issued police press notice. The notice had been released immediately after the arrest, so it had been in planning for some time. It wasn't on Nicky's radar because the minor nature of the arrest warrant hadn't needed to be flagged up to her level, as it was so very far removed from what they were 'investigating'. Raby was arrested for money laundering and witness intimidation, still worth a good eighteen months in jail. The end of a not-so-impressive career as a policeman and off-the-radar paedophile. The police press notice hadn't mentioned that part. They obviously didn't know. Well, they would soon.

Chris was extremely relieved when he received an instant message back from MB, who seemed to take it in her stride. But he couldn't shake the feeling that it would rear its ugly head again before this was over.

Chapter Forty-Four

Lucia was having a very nice late supper at the Dorchester Hotel in Central London when the encrypted e-mail pinged once, then locked shut the iPhone 5 (pre-release version) with its new 128-bit random code keyed security. It couldn't be opened unless you had a paired synchronised random code generator. These keys were issued on an individual basis and cost just over half a million dollars each. The FBI were livid with Silicon Valley for developing a tool able to protect criminals, terrorists and paedophiles worldwide. Lucia did not give it a second thought. She was only interested in her personal protection for her little project.

She slipped away from the table and headed into the ladies' powder room. Once sitting comfortably in the plush stall, she put in the earpiece while she viewed the video Christopher had sent. She was glad she had, for the police car sirens were loud. The shouted commands during the arrest could be nothing but real. It also included the police press notice. She smiled. That fool, Raby, had got himself arrested on some minor charges. Christopher would not have the opportunity to get to him before June 14, her deadline, her unbreakable anniversary. The thought of her father in her arms, in their shared bed, on that day, made her heart feel lighter. That was the day he had given her Catalina, and why it held such bittersweet memories. Now her unnatural smile was more genuine; it even reached one of her eyes. She didn't even notice that the other unsmiling eye was violently twitching ever so slightly. She could easily get to Raby in any prison or police cell – that's what her little B's were for – whenever she decided, and she decided it would be soon.

She quickly e-mailed Christopher telling him not to worry about Raby. It would give him a false sense of hope. But she told him to make sure he killed the teacher, Emma Brumby-Smith, only on Thursday, June 14, before noon, or his family would pay the ultimate price. Actually, she said she would kill them slowly, and very painfully. She did so enjoy planting disturbing images in his head.

Lucia was, however, starting to grudgingly respect him for his initiative, ingenuity, and bloody-minded determination. All those beautiful kills, on self-incriminating videos to boot, to be used at a later date, and still no arrest – clever boy.

She exited the stall and had the Puerto Rican attendant wash, dry and moisturise her hands. She thanked her in Spanish, dropping a £50 note into the sink; as a tip, yes, but for the most part, so she wouldn't be remembered. This was an unspoken agreement with every housekeeper, porter, bellboy, concierge and attendant she ever met.

On her return to the table, her thoughts turned to Juanita and her little charges. Lucia hadn't unlocked the door for four days so they should be out of food by now. Hunger can be its own form of torture. Poor Juanita was expecting better from Lucia right up until she had pulled Juanita's one remaining tooth out with pliers. The dashed expectation only made Lucia enjoy her own meal even more. Maybe tomorrow Sophie and Matilda would also enjoy a meal. Maybe, but only because their own deadline was looming and she had a little surprise for Christopher when he turned up at the Mayfair house. She fully expected him to, for she was allowing one of the hackers to slowly locate it, but only on her terms. He would turn up and die, along with his beautiful family. The house would become the Beem mausoleum.

Chapter Forty-Five

The whole of Team Beem concentrated intently on the video-conference call, which had been convened at short notice. Sketchley walked everyone through the facts as they stood right up to date. Team paedo were all in lockdown at Base Waddington, except Raby who was in lockdown in lockup, safe, sound and happily uncomfortable in the local nick. Coppers hated bent coppers more than villains. Well, nearly.

Sketchley outlined the sequence of events for the next four days. They had all worked towards this climax for six weeks. Thursday would be June 14 and no one was under any illusions as to its significance. They had all seen the information about the General and his daughter, Lucia.

Nicky reminded all present that despite the fact they were going to put on one spectacular show for MB (Nicky had asked if they could call her Lucia now, but it humanised her too much, so NO), there could be no collateral damage. Property was acceptable but no civilians or innocent bystanders could get even a scratch.

She had placed a trusted team of loyal officers on stand-by for rapid deployment and had set an operational briefing for 07:00 hours on Thursday. Officers would be in place, primed and ready. Nicky confirmed the police had contained the flow of information, internal and external, with their story holding up under the usual scrutiny both upstairs and across the rank and file.

The press was happily not in possession of the full facts. Well, any facts, actually.

Nicky was able to confirm that whilst working with Fido and Sketchley, they had made 1500 connections in the Midlands alone.

Sketchley and Nicky had grown a little closer during their post-planning late suppers, during which they had been collating a file for Interpol and the FBI. It had a disturbing 26,000 names on it worldwide; this group had been active for at least thirty years. The Base Waddington group were looking at 100 years+ jail time for their crimes. The publicity for this alone would swell the police ranks, which was good, as recruitment was at an all-time low.

Fido told the group he was closing in on the address of the final safe house. They had identified some locations through the IP addresses and were slowly getting through the firewall one step at a time. He told the group that the Rev's laptop had been a goldmine; without it, they would still know nothing about this group.

He confirmed he had three specialists who had been briefed only on the search, capture/kill of MB (Lucia Maria Domingo), and the safe retrieval of Sophie and Tilly. They were in two teams in case MB was holding the girls in a separate location to her own. He would lead one, with Mick (no nickname) Hynan, a former paratrooper and specialist tracker, to lead the other.

Freddy told the team he had prepared arrest warrants for Gabriel Raby, Emma Brumby-Smith, the Reverend Dr Noah Morris-Hargreaves, Mercer Dayton and Jerel Jamar.

Charge one: Sexual Assault and Buggery. Contrary to Section 12 of the Sexual Offences Act 1956.

Along with a shocking revelation.

Charge Two: Murder. Contrary to Common Law, for the vicious murder of MB's own daughter, Catalina. This stunned everyone into asking questions all at once. However, he did not want to go into the particulars. Due to the sensitive nature of the offences, they would need delicate handling. Suffice it to say, the Rev's laptop had provided all the indisputable evidence they would ever need against the whole group. It contained disturbing images and videos too explicit for this call, but they identified all of them beyond any shadow of a doubt. It was a slam dunk for the CPS.

Chris thanked the group for all their help and continued support, reminding them not to leave anything to chance. Nothing could go wrong. There was just too much at stake.

His final target was Brumby-Smith, the teacher. She was possibly the worst of them all, breaking all known laws of man and nature, and the trust of the victims. She lured young girls and boys to be violated, grooming the vulnerable for the worst type of abuse, finding the defenceless, and pitching the victims, including Catalina, to the group, all for the money.

Brumby-Smith may not have gotten involved in the abuse, but she was the cause of it all. If the evidence wasn't compelling enough, in a sickening twist, she was also a teacher at the same school attended by Tilly. Chris wished he could kill her for real. Just the thought of what could have happened made him shake with rage.

They were all sure of their roles in Thursday's events, but the timings were crucial.

He relayed what MB had confirmed – his family were safe for now and being well cared for, but he reiterated the not-so-veiled threat.

Full steam ahead to the finale.

Chapter Forty-Six

Chris set off from Base Waddington's 24/7/365 paedophile storage facility on the road to the final chapter. Still cautious, he headed back to Lincoln via Newark which would take twice as long, but where there was one Bosnian WWF goon, there was potential for many. It was essential that Base Waddington remained a secret.

The plan was ready, the team were ready, and the in-house cops were ready.

As he drove the convoluted route, he thought about his own family and the dread he had been living with for the last adrenaline-fuelled ten weeks. How he wished he had taken a different direction for his morning run that day – although, now knowing most of what Lucia had put him through, he was sure this nightmare would be happening despite his actions that cold April morning. He believed he would have also gone mad if he had suffered as Lucia had, but it didn't give her the right to hurt Sophie or Tilly. Him, maybe, but them, never.

So here he was at 0600 hours on June 14, 2012, exactly thirty years to the day since, as part of his role during operation 'Snake's Head', he had shot and deliberately killed the General. On that cold, windy day, over difficult terrain from his unobserved observation post situated on the lee side of the mountain overlooking the occupied Port Stanley, it took only a single shot, fired over 658 metres at 2,600 feet per second to do the job. That combat action had brought him here today, heading back to Lincoln to kill Brumby-Smith. His route took him via Retford, twenty miles west of Lincoln, which is where his tail picked him up. However, this time Chris was hoping it would happen. It would save him valuable time driving around, trying to find a rent-a-goon to play tag with.

Chris could not humanize MB by calling her Lucia, even in his head. She had demanded that Brumby-Smith's death be both spectacular and visual, obviously in the clear hope he would be caught in the act. But he had other ideas...

Fido and his international team of professional soldiers were closing in on her. They had narrowed her current IP address down to just three locations: one in Mayfair, a former embassy; one on the South Bank near the London Eye, a former council chambers with forty rooms; and the final one, a Gothic-style, eight-bedroomed place in Pall Mall.

Fido had chosen the Mayfair embassy residence for no other reason than that he liked the location; it meant he could have dinner at Scott's, which was one of his favourite London restaurants.

Chris, however, had an altogether different decision to make and he was running out of time to make it. Should he alert Nicky of his plan to appear to blow Brumby-Smith up so she could be there to arrest her? Maybe she should know because it was going to create a shit storm the likes of which Lincoln had never seen, and hopefully would never see again. However, having basically invited his enemy to the ball, he didn't want to draw the attention of any of MB's rent-a-goons to a massive police activity prior to the event. He knew Nicky would definitely not appreciate the big bang approach and was sure to put a stop to it. She had already warned about collateral damage, even without knowing his plan. But he didn't have an alternative and he had taken the time and a lot of trouble to make this look real. One false move and it could blow the whole gig. But if there wasn't a police presence, things could go spectacularly wrong and end up with the wrong people being arrested.

Chapter Forty-Seven

Everything was finally in place. Lights, camera, action. Clapperboard down, positions, please. Take one and only one. No rehearsals, no repeats. Chris was actually shaking and his mouth was cotton dry. He could see goon one and goon two from his vantage point. He could also see Brumby-Smith strolling to her car without a care in the world – that was going to change very quickly. He couldn't see Nicky or her team, thank God! However, he knew she was there, along with Freddy, hopefully mob-handed, with a thick blue line ready for the takedown.

Time: T minus five minutes and counting.

He pinged all parties, who were waiting with the same bated breath for the final act, for the curtain to fall. *Enough with the theatrical metaphors*, he thought, despite considering them all very apt.

Brumby-Smith continued her casual stroll, whilst texting or tweeting, towards her car in the left quarter of Westgate East car park. She appeared completely unaware that the car park was unusually half-empty and other pedestrians were surprisingly scarce – a precaution Nicky had insisted upon – and didn't even notice her car was completely isolated in its lonely corner. Actually, it had been moved to three spaces. You would notice if you were looking, but she wasn't. She never was.

Chris was in position at the top of the 120-foot-tall Westgate Water Tower, completed in 1911, built due to the 1904 typhoid outbreak. It offered an uninterrupted 360-degree vantage point.

He had set up three high-definition cameras: one next to him, one on the castle wall pointing directly at Brumby-Smith's car, and one on the antique shop roof opposite the car park, covering a wider angle. He wanted MB to see the action in real-time because there would only be a very short window of opportunity for her to be convinced all had gone to plan. At least, the part of the plan Chris had told her about via the usual communication link. A bonus was that the goons had no doubt already reported in whilst they were sitting comfortably in their hire cars at the far end of the car park. They had occupied this slot for the last three days. They were even side by side, a massive tactical error. Another tactical error was in the location. Parking there meant they had their backs to the rear, pedestrian-only entrance, which they clearly didn't know about. Just beyond the said pedestrian entrance, Nicky and Freddy were in an unmarked, wholesale meat delivery van, along with eight handpicked, heavily armed SCO19 firearms officers and a police sergeant, who were all poised ready to make the arrests.

Right now, Brumby-Smith was fiddling with the keys on her Save the Panda keyring, ready to press the automatic door opener. She slipped easily into the driver's seat. Although it did feel a little higher than usual, she didn't take any notice and simply adjusted the rear-view mirror to match the adjustment in height.

Brumby-Smith had just pushed the starter button with her left hand when a blue flash seemed to reach out as if to gently stroke it.

Chris double-checked there was no one in the blast zone and pressed the metaphorical red button. It was actually a single-digit number on his phone which triggered the bomb.

He was looking through the viewfinder of the HD camera, which was also the same view MB was seeing. Suddenly,

Brumby-Smith's car seemed to jump vertically twenty feet into the air and immediately disassemble itself, instantly dispersing its body parts over the whole corner of Westgate car park. It emitted a sound which can only be described as a massive, earth-shattering, ear-splitting explosion or more generally known as a fucking big bang.

Brumby-Smith was not feeling any of the sensations you would normally expect to feel whilst having your car blown up because she was dead.

Chapter Forty-Eight

Chris did not wait around to see what effect the explosion was having on Lincoln and its population. He was too busy abseiling down the north face of the water tower, out of view of the car park. He wanted to get to Brumby-Smith's car, or what remained of it, before anyone else, including MB's goons who may or may not yet be under arrest. He also needed to get there before any police, not on Nicky's tag team, and therefore not in position of the full facts. As agreed with Nicky, he should remove all the incriminating evidence, mainly the cameras, but particularly the homemade car taser kit. That would be hard for Freddy to explain away once it was entered into evidence.

He had killed the live feed from the cameras seconds after the car had finished disassembling itself and sending its parts across the car park. He quickly arrived at what remained of a once rather nice pastel-blue Peugeot 208, only to find a smouldering rubberised cage complete with Brumby-Smith, dead to the world, inside. Apart from suffering a few bloodied scratches, singed hair, complete loss of eyebrows, massive shock, a splitting headache and a lifetime of tinnitus, she would survive! She was out for the count, so he didn't bother to give her any ketamine hydrochloride.

Nicky, along with two determined-looking SCO19 officers, were just seconds away. Brumby-Smith was motionless, ready for the cuffs and a mercifully long prison sentence. She had permanently been removed from society with the biggest of big bangs.

While the mayhem continued around him, Chris headed off, at a quick jog, to the waiting Skoda parked between the magnificent and aptly named Tower Hotel, and the actual water tower. There, a patient but exhausted SK was waiting to take them down to London to join Fido, who should have news by the time they arrived. As they drove, they discussed the last three days and reflected on what a success the high-risk strategy had been.

In the run-up to blowing the shit out of Brumby-Smith's Peugeot 208, SK had permanently borrowed the same make and model from the East Midlands Airport's long-stay car park. Examining this enabled them to know the exact dimensions of the interior, and how all the external panels connected and reacted to pressure points. They discovered what they could blow up and what areas to protect so it didn't become the fireball from hell. It had taken days to work out exactly how to add crumpled joints to fixed parts, tethering the panels so they didn't fly across the car park and endanger anyone, and how to move them out of the way using remote-controlled drop bolts so they did not become lethal objects. All this preparation was for a Hollywood-style explosion; all noise, smoke and mirrors, with a few splashes of artificial blood for good measure.

Once they were sure this could be done safely, after much deliberation, they fully committed to an explosive end to all this. They had swapped Brumby-Smith's original driver's seat for a custom-made blast-proof Kevlar uvex phynomic x-foam seat with instant expanding flame-resistant neoprene. This was designed to absorb all the energy from the blast whilst keeping Brumby-Smith cocooned in her new space-age seat on loan from East Midlands Airport.

They had rigged the car's interior to be propelled upwards five feet first, and then for only the tethered outer skin of the car's bodywork to be blown outwards, away from the driver. Like Michael Caine, they had indeed intended to blow the bloody doors off, but unlike him, they had achieved just that. They even managed to keep the blast zone to twenty-four mostly unoccupied parking bays, with all the explosives pre-set to push energy outwards, thus creating one spectacular detonation whilst minimising the risk, not eliminating it completely, but a risk they were more than prepared to take for this scumbag child recruiter.

Brumby-Smith had been blissfully unaware of any of the events leading up to her arrest. She had been zapped by the blue flash, which was, in fact, Chris' custom-made remote-controlled car taser. Shocking but true. He now had it safely in the rear of the Skoda, along with some expensive mini-HD cameras which SK was going to return, but to where, he didn't know.

Once cut free from the now fully expanded neoprene seat, a dazed, smoking Brumby-Smith was duly cautioned and arrested by Freddy Three Fingers and Nicky Nails for littering. Oh, and for being a paedophile, and a child-snatching scumbag murderer.

She was arrested along with the two carelessly parked goons, who she had never met but was going to be formally introduced to in the back of the Black Maria any minute now.

As they drove on to their destiny, Chris glanced over at SK and for the first time in a long time, he took a moment to marvel at his efforts. This one-man dynamo had been amazing and put himself through so much, solely to help Chris and his family. He had never, for a second, questioned Chris' actions, never lost an ounce of faith in all they were doing, and continually put himself in harm's way, with a possible arrest at any time. He had willingly committed a lot of small crimes and quite a few larger ones.

He was the best friend anyone could possibly get, and when this was finally all over, Chris would tell him that, in no uncertain terms. This was one friendship he would never again let slip into the annals of time. He felt a true, loving connection, never before experienced outside his immediate family.

Chapter Forty-Nine

Lucia was dancing around in the second-floor reception room. She was like a giddy schoolgirl after her first litre of dry cider. The live video feed she had just been watching, in all its explosive glory, was sensational in every detail. She had not even minded when the explosion had made her drop the vintage crystal wine goblet, with its 1982 Chateau Lafite Rothschild now wasting away soaking into her Persian rug. She didn't even curse when she gently picked it up and refilled it with the ruby red elixir of life. She had been dreaming of this day for a decade or more; it had been in her conscious thought every waking moment of every day since Catalina had been buried in a lonely corner of her South American exile. Punishing the killers of her beautiful daughter, galvanised by the double joy of punishing the murderer of her beloved father, gave her pleasure in equal measure. It was a heady cocktail of revenge, even more so knowing Christopher would never get his prize. A prize which would remain as elusive as she was about to become.

This was simply perfect. All the paedophiles are dead, or soon to be. She had taken all the necessary measures to have Raby killed in prison. It would cost her a lot of money, but it was worth it.

Lucia was talking to herself loudly now. It didn't matter that no one was there to hear her.

Christopher, the poor soon-to-be widower, was also soon to be in jail, for if the police did not catch him, she would provide the full and frank dossier against him herself. She wouldn't hesitate in giving them the step-by-step guide, in graphic gory video form, as evidence – the killer in action.

She would send them anonymously to Chief Constable Charles Davey, who had been in the news with reference to Dayton recently, appealing for witnesses.

Lucia shouted loudly, to no one in particular, "Never mind, here's a break in the case for you, Mr Davey. A serial killer in HD."

She refilled her glass and placed it on the table next to her .357 Magnum. It was loaded and cocked ready, just in case any little B's came a-buzzing, looking for long-lost comrades or retribution.

She had packed days ago, knowing she would need to be out of here in the next hour or so – she had left enough clues to her location. Christopher must be driving here by now. It would only take three hours, so she would be gone by 2 p.m. She had a private flight booked from the City Airport to Schiphol where she was meeting Zejneba (B1). He wanted payment for Raby up front, which would conclude their little project. After that, onwards to Chile and once there, it was only a quick hop to home – safe and sound, no extradition possible.

She hadn't heard from B5 or B8. She smiled because she had always known all their silly little individual names; Ademij and Ahilej, respectively. She hoped Christopher had killed them, or the police had. That would save her a million dollars.

Not many loose ends now. She was surprised she had not felt that euphoria longer, that she had not felt freer from her mental-emotional straight jacket.

Maybe she would when that *bastardo*, Laser, realised that even after all he had done, he had not saved Sophie or Matilda.

Maybe his pain and anguish would be the nectar which she craved, serenity for her soul. She cursed herself for speaking his name in this house.

Lucia's eye was twitching so badly now that she was having to rub it just to be able to see straight. She paced around the room, rubbing her tired temples, thinking, *Why am I not free? Why am I not happy?* All the while, she was losing track of time, while she was also losing track of her mind.

Lucia giggled to herself. In fact, she was laughing so hard now that she was on the very edge of hysteria. She had only ever known true love at the hands of her father, his loving caresses making her feel beautiful, needed, and special, finally giving her the ultimate gift, a daughter, her beautiful daughter.

She slapped her own face hard; she knew she had to get control of her rage, which threatened to overpower her. These flights of fancy, making her slip back into the very memories which tormented her, must stop.

She must store these thoughts for another time when she was safely away from all this.

Just when she could take it no longer, an almighty crash brought her back down to earth. Lucia reacted quickly, grabbing the handgun from the elegant side table, and knocking the crystal goblet onto the carpet once more. This time it was staying there.

She slipped into a man-made recess cut directly into the stone wall beside the enormous ornate Victorian fireplace. Then she was gone.

Chapter Fifty

Fido and his team had rendezvoused at the Mayfair mansion, having eliminated the other sites, mainly by breaking and entering them.

Fido was now certain he had the right house; he was sure it was MB he had seen pacing frantically around in an upstairs room, laughing hysterically and shouting obscenities in Spanish. He had seen the file and knew she was Argentinian by birth. It all made a perverse kind of sense to him now.

Fido was worried she was now so unhinged that no matter what Chris did, she was going to kill his family anyway. Fido fucking hated clichés, but this was not going to happen on his watch. Chris had entrusted the safe return of his girls to him and his team, a responsibility that he took seriously. Actually, with his life, kind of seriously. He knew the whole of the Beem team felt the same. It wasn't about the paedos; it was family, pure and simple. Although the paedo thing helped their conscience, a lot!

Fido had three weapons experts with him and all the equipment they would need to breach the mansion in quick time, in complete silence, and with a minimum of fuss, which was what they were doing right now.

Fuck! The second entrance door was crudely, but effectively, booby-trapped with, believe it or not, a set of Medieval armour, which clattered to the marble floor. Once started on the downward trajectory, it simply could not be stopped, making one almighty crash, bang, wallop. The helmet clattered across the floor like a medieval bowling ball.

Once inside, No Nickname, along with Yogi (Simon Bear), bounded up the magnificent sweeping staircase, still in stealth mode. They were hoping to capture/kill (he hadn't promised Freddy shit) MB. Having studied the floor plans of this 300-year-old mansion, Fido knew there was a large underground cellar and he headed there with Dinger (Andrew Bell). What better place to hide anything of value? Safe-deposit boxes, gold, paintings, expensive wine – and hostages, obviously.

Fido led the search; Dinger stood guard. Slowly, with every sinew as taut as double bass strings, he crept through the massive vaulted-ceiling cellar, following some dusty footprints until he came to a brick wall where they ended abruptly. Fido could see the prints went into the wall, ergo, it wasn't a real wall, or it wasn't fixed in place – the whole hidden room trick. He had played these games before, so knew they could be dangerous, especially if the opponent was well motivated; and MB was, by her own actions, very well motivated.

He applied all his logic. He knew from bitter experience how painful contempt for your opponent could prove to be, so he showed this problem proper respect. He observed a high level of caution, knowing it would be a bloody disaster to rush in, just to get caught, thumb up the bum, mind in neutral, completely off guard, which was basically all the same thing, and equally embarrassing for a professional like Fido.

With twenty paces left, there was a 90-degree, angled recess in the wall where a keyhole was prominent. It was invisible from anywhere except close up, at a 45-degrees angle. *Clever design,* thought Fido, *but not clever enough.* He had brought with him a universal skeleton key which was able to open all but the most sophisticated locks. For them, he had a powerful hand-held diamond drill and a portable butane gas blowtorch. Nothing stood up to raw power, but he wanted the element of surprise for what or who lay on the other side of this secret wall. You didn't go to all this trouble not to have your own surprise waiting, and he was sure it wasn't going to be a nice surprise – no party poppers, no champagne, only pain.

He slid the whole wall slowly along well-greased tracks which made no sound at all. He gave a nod to the engineers who had put this false wall in place; it must have weighed two tons at least, but still no sound. It was also soundproofed; however, he still took it a centimetre at a time, being mindful of booby traps. Today's combat zones, whether it was Afghanistan, Iraq, or Mayfair, were potentially full of IEDs which could kill or maim. Then it really would be the end game. So Fido took his time, which was how he found the tripwire which, in turn, was attached to a Claymore.

A bloody Claymore! A free-standing, omnidirectional anti-personnel mine, which causes the worst type of damage imaginable. It was pointing directly at the entrance, covering ninety degrees. The pin was removed, primed ready to reduce everyone in a 100-metre radius to shredded bags of human garbage. These were lethal devices, proving MB did not hold life as sacred. The mad bitch.

Fido knew that while the safety pin was in place, as it was now, he had used his matchstick. It was completely safe to walk past but he remained vigilant at all times. There could be many more devices. Luckily for Fido, MB's hiring policy wasn't as stringent as his. She had hired really lazy bastards – there was only one deterrent.

He reached the metal cages in no time at all. He could see the locks were still in place, and the tatty blankets were piled on the comfy-looking, but filthy mattresses. There was only one empty bucket for human waste but surprisingly, there were two toilet seats. He wondered what had happened to the other bucket. But there was nothing else. No Sophie, no Tilly, both cages empty. He supposed it would have been too easy to find them at the first attempt.

The only life in the room was a large swarm of black meat flies which were continually circling the lifeless body of a little, old, leather-skinned woman. Her completely toothless jaw lay open and slack, probably in shock at being shot – there was a single bullet hole in the centre of her forehead. The only surprising thing about the whole scene was that she had what looked like a single new shiny white porcelain tooth, inserted halfway into the gaping head wound.

If this was some kind of visual metaphor, it was lost on Fido and Dinger.

Chapter Fifty-One

Freddy and Nicky stood with their SCO19 team, along with Wing Commander Keith Dolby OBE DFC, at the Base Waddington compounds spring camp for paedophiles. Having received an anonymous, wink-wink tip-off, they were going over the jam-packed file in all its gloriously detailed content, including the inventory of the paedophile ring and their crimes. When this was all over, they would have to offer Sketchley a job. *What an asset he would make, and a pretty good companion, too*, thought Nicky.

They scanned the room, amused that the remaining group were currently in cages wearing their very own rubber S&M suits, now fully zipped up at both ends, handcuffed to their individual beds, complete with an en suite bucket in the corner. Evidently, SK had given up on the niceties of cage life once he had found out about their real sexual proclivities. He had even switched off the heaters. Nicky doubted this group would ever solicit any personal sympathies ever again.

The dossier which Sketchley had collated was complete with every scrap of information the police would need, including the self-incriminating laptop passwords. It also contained a detailed account of Chris and his team's own actions, so Freddy would have time to prepare any counter measures ready for the inevitable fallout from his own superiors, or to write his own criminal charge sheets for Mr Christopher (Laser) Beem or Mr Phillip (Sketchley) Clarke, depending on how he saw it.

Freddy would be handling the press explosion, including the inevitable selfish grandstanding intrusions into everything, including the family's lives. He would not allow them to devalue the victims and use disgusting unnecessarily salacious reporting, just to sell a few more papers.

His job now was to protect the victims, at all costs.

Nicky, whilst being appalled at everything which had transpired, had to admit that she and Freddy were absolutely amazed too. Chris had pulled off this astonishing feat, having effectively captured, not killed, an entire paedophile ring which was secretly located on her own bloody doorstep. It was an audacious plan which could have backfired at any moment, pitting him against the law, at the same time as losing his whole family.

Freddy and Nicky quietly agreed that they would do everything in their power to keep him free from prosecution, and therefore, by association, the complete team, which actually included both of them. A pass on moral grounds, if not on any known lawful ones. Good guys: 6. Paedophiles: 0.

While Chris and SK raced down to London to meet Fido, Nicky said a silent prayer, imploring God to help Chris find his family safe. At the same time, if he didn't mind, please protect Sketchley, too. She had unintentionally grown very fond of that funny, easily underestimated little man.

Freddy texted Chris to tell him he wasn't going to appear in court, he wasn't going to be anybody's star witness, as long as he kept the solemn promise he had made to Freddy from the outset – not to exact any type of personal revenge. He must not murder Lucia. He must trust Freddy and let justice prevail.

Freddy had worked out a plausible hypothesis, with just enough information to let everyone, hierarchy, press included, read between the lines and fill in the gaps themselves if they didn't look too hard. It was fortunate that Nicky just happened to be on the phone to Gold Command when the 'wink-wink' tip-off came in. Anyway, who was going to start digging around when it came to removing six paedophiles permanently from society? Even the most politically correct police-hating press could never begin to defend these types. This group was, as they say, bang to rights.

Police Inspector Gabriel Raby, who was already in police custody, saw his charge sheet swiftly change from low-level crime to never seeing the light of day again in the time it had taken Freddy to sign his name.

Teacher, Emma Louise Brumby-Smith, had been whisked extremely quickly and relatively painlessly (mores the pity), to the local A&E, leaving a smoking vapour trail the Red Arrows would have been proud of.

Post her flying visit to the hospital, she was now in handcuffs, in a police cell. Her charge sheet was for procuring minors for sexual gratification (it was a lot wordier), but the littering charge had to be dropped – they had run out of space on the form! She, too, would never see the light of day again.

The clergyman – the Subdean of the Lincolnshire dioceses – Reverend Dr Noah William Morris-Hargreaves was in bed one. He would have loved the rubber suit normally, but the prospect of prison had put a damper on his ardour, somewhat. A lifetime in jail charges to follow.

Businessman and High Sheriff Connor Laurence Mercer was in bed two. The team were sure he had wet himself at the mention of the police because his left foot was three times its normal size, the liquid having nowhere else to go. A lifetime in jail charges to follow.

The builder, Nathan John Dayton of FossWay Commercial Construction, was in bed three. If he could see clearly, he would not be happy with the build quality of these cages. A lifetime in jail charges to follow.

Last, but not least, the chef, Jerel Martin Jamar, was amazingly asleep in bed number four, or so it appeared. A lifetime in jail; charges to follow, just like all the rest. All the others were trying to plead for freedom. Well, Nicky assumed that was what they were trying to do, but no one could really tell, only hearing muffled squeaks through their masked faces. The time would come, soon enough, for protestations of innocence, but with all the evidence, it would thankfully fall on deaf ears. All proceeds of their crimes would be confiscated so they wouldn't be able to afford fancy lawyers, either.

Freddy took control of the soon-to-be guests of Her Majesty the Queen.

He also prayed that Chris, SK and Fido would have the same level of success in London. He wanted Chris to have his long-awaited and very hard-earned reunion with Sophie and Tilly.

Chapter Fifty-Two

Fido, No Nickname, and his team of battle-hardened international mercenaries were visibly shaken by the empty cages. Notably, they were not at all shaken by the dead body, just annoyed at all the flies.

No Nickname and his team had done an exhaustive room-by-room search, top to bottom, roof to cellar.

As this was clearly the only place in the house which Sophie and Tilly had actually been, they all set about a fingertip search of the room for any signs of life, any clues to the girls' whereabouts, but nothing. Not a sausage, not a red bean. Fuck all.

Fido leaned against the back wall of the cellar for a breather; the tension was sucking all the air out of the room. They had cleared the other two residences they had located on the computer. They too were clean as a whistle. They had actually slept at the Pall Mall one the prior evening. He was just about to give up looking any further in this room and abandon it for an intensive search up the stairs, when the wall seemed to vibrate ever so slightly, almost imperceptibly, but shimmer it did, giving them a glimmer of hope.

Fido immediately tasked everyone with an inch-by-inch search of the wall for any hidden mechanisms which would allow it to move. It looked, for all intents and purposes, like the structural load-bearing wall it should be, joining both houses together. But they had nearly been fooled once getting into this room, so they were not taking anything for granted – no stone, or brick, untouched. So, inch by slow meticulous painstaking inch, they all searched. The hours crawled by and they discovered nothing, a big fat zero, zilch, nada, fuck all.

Chris and SK could not get Fido on the phone. They wondered whether they were in an area with no signal, but that seemed unlikely as their last know location was Mayfair in Central London, noted for excellent cellular service.

Chris was a little worried because this had been the only part of his and SK's detailed plan which was out of his immediate control. He couldn't be in two places at once, obviously. He'd had to delegate the massive responsibility for his family's safety to Fido. Not that he had any concerns about Fido, God no, nor his fantastic team. He was genuinely worried about the unpredictable nature of MB. She may well live up to her name and just kill Sophie and Tilly out of spite, malice, or simply just being mad. Maybe she had never really intended to let them go free.

He had a strange far-off feeling that regardless of the massive hoops which he had jumped through, she was clearly as mad as a March hare. Firstly, she had clearly harboured all this hate for him for thirty years. Yes, he had killed her father, but as a wholly sanctioned act of war, not as a personal vendetta. That, combined with the senseless, brutal killing of her daughter – coincidentally in his hometown – had been too much for her, seemingly fracturing her mind. He could see he was her focal point and she wanted him to suffer. On reflection, while he had been looking at her on that HD TV, he recalled she had been twitching, and the silly little smirk followed by the full-blown evil long-distance stare had shown her madness. There was no way of telling what would happen next.

He hoped Fido would ring any second now, putting them out of their misery with good news. It would also mean he had not told a bare-faced lie to Freddy and would not be going to hell after all.

Meanwhile, No Nickname had found an astonishing piece of structural engineering. He had noticed four of the bricks had fingerprints embedded in the chalk dust, naturally created from movement within the cellar. Only four bricks had fingerprints; the rest of the wall was wiped clean. He pressed them in turn – nothing. He pressed in a random pattern – nothing. All at the same time – nothing. He assigned them numbers – brick 1, brick 2, brick 3 and brick 4 – then pressed them in different sequences, 1234, 4321, 1111, 3333, 2222, 4444, 2244, 3344, 2233, etc. He was just about to give up when Fido told him about when Chris was trying to open the rucksack with a combination. So, as a last-ditch effort, 3, 8, 1 and 1 for luck. Hey, presto! Open Sesame! The combination released a hidden locking mechanism and allowed the whole wall to rotate on a central axle. Ingenious! It would have remained hidden forever if the hired help had only cleaned the bricks thoroughly.

Behind the wall, Fido and his team found a secret passage which led to the next house. They searched both houses between them and came up empty-handed. They stayed at the task for hours, the search becoming more panicked by the minute. Fido only broke off the search to inform Chris of his progress, or lack of it. Chris was now only ten minutes away.

Fido asked everyone to once again methodically search from the cellar to the roof tiles, inch by inch, room by room, floor by floor. Thus, several hours later, they had been through both residences with a fine-tooth comb. By this time, Chris and SK had also arrived and joined in. Then, when Fido's exhausted team took a break, Chris and SK did a complete top-to-bottom search themselves. Not that they didn't trust Fido. It was like looking for your car keys in an empty box and returning time and time again to the empty box, expecting them to have magically appeared. Their search was not out of expectation, but out of hope. They knew Sophie and Tilly weren't magically going to appear, but they had to try. Any little bit of hope, anything to point them towards his family, for Christ's sake, anything would do. It didn't have to be a burning bush or a hand-written sign from God, a fingernail or, God forbid, a blood splatter, just any small thing. *Please, please, anything*, was all Chris could hold in his now completely frazzled head.

It was only his personal willpower which was keeping him from losing it completely. It was his belief in family and loyalty which had gotten him this far. This couldn't be the end. He had to keep fighting or lose everything by default, so he started again, in the cellar.

Sketchley, on the other hand, was sitting in the ground floor reception room, completely exhausted, taking five minutes to recharge, to decompress. He had been running on empty for the best part of eight weeks, driven not by a selfish personal agenda, but for comradeship; out of loyalty, out of respect, out of love. His driver was to find Sophie and Matilda. This motivation had spurred him on even more than he had realised. He now knew he wanted a family to call his own, his own loyal dependable wife and a couple of loved and loving children. Not much to ask, but although it was all he had ever really wanted, he knew it was too late for that now. The fact he had nothing prior to this adventure only highlighted he still had nothing worth going home to; a shitty flat, abject matrimony-driven poverty, no job, no prospects. Well, until recently, that was. Maybe, just maybe, there was a small light at the end of the tunnel. Just maybe Nicky was holding it up for him. Well, he could dream, couldn't he?

Although he was not the kind of guy to let anyone down – never had, never would, never will – he was so tired he could hardly stand, so he was having five minutes. That's all, just five minutes to rest, in peace.

A single shot rang out. Sketchley hadn't actually heard the shot because he was the recipient of the bullet. It killed him instantly, right where he sat.

Lucia had crept out of her recently renovated priest hole and fired her .357 Magnum handgun, more as a distraction. She had no idea who she had shot. She just wanted to make sure it was loud, creating an opportunity through the commotion, to slip silently out through the front door. The commotion had everyone else in the building naturally rushing, weapons drawn, in the opposite direction, to offer protection and administer aid to Sketchley. Sadly, this would prove to be both ineffective and way too late. This would be SK's final resting place.

Once the team had regrouped and regained their senses, they dashed out the main door, keeping their weapons out of sight. There was no sight of MB or anyone else for that matter, including any police activity. The age and thick stone walls of the house had deadened the gunshot. This would buy them the time to continue searching, even in vain. This was not over yet.

Fido, No Nickname and Yogi rolled up SK, as gently as was possible, on the Persian rug and placed him in the Skoda. They would get Freddy's advice on their best next action.

"Free rug," said Dinger. Military humour was always macabre during times of stress. It did, however, relieve the tension.

The team had to admit defeat. MB was in the wind, on her

toes. She had spirited herself away. She was gone, but not forgotten. They all had to admit they would never catch up with her, especially if she had boarded a private jet. SK had recently learnt there was one sitting, prepped and ready at London City Airport. They did not have any authority to arrest or even detain her. Freddy and Nicky were still tidying up the aftermath of their Lincoln adventure and would not be able to get an arrest warrant in time, anyway.

What haunted Fido the most was it had only taken ten extra minutes to find where MB had been hiding. How had they messed it up so badly? How had they missed the priest hole? After all, they were professionals. They weren't bloody professionals on this evidence.

Chapter Fifty-Three

Chris had taken himself away from the rest of the team to the uppermost room of the very grand house. He wanted privacy, and needed solitude, knowing he would not be able to contain his emotions. Despite the years of domestication, he was still too macho to let the others see what he knew was coming. Sitting alone in the empty room, farthest away from the commotion down the stairs, feeling the abject misery of the whole sorry situation, he cried for only the third time in forty years: Tilly's birth, the loss of his family in Cornwall, and now, the senseless killing of his best friend, Sketchley.

He must have been sitting there for more than two hours. His head ached and his bloodshot eyes watered from the outpouring of grief. Even after all this, he still hadn't found his girls. Rubbing his eyes with the palms of his hands, he sat there considering making the now gargantuan effort required to make a move. He noticed a small fresh puddle of very yellow liquid which must have just been formed by a very slow, but near-constant, dripping from the ceiling. He couldn't immediately see any hatch, not even one you might associate with a loft or other access point to the roof.

Remembering what Fido and Dinger had told him in detail about the hidden rooms in the cellar and the adjacent basement, he sat patiently watching.

Plop.

Then, fifteen minutes later, it happened again. Another drip, plop. Then, after twenty minutes, eventually another. Something was permeating the ceiling. Although he still didn't realise it, it was a bigger fucking sign than any amount of burning bushes.

Chris called down to the others and they all stared at the…

Drip…

Drip…

Drip…

Drip… and each yellow drip was full of nothing but hope.

Fido had retrieved a stepladder, just long enough to reach the high Victorian ceiling, and was once again conducting a fingertip search. He was not bloody surprised to find the hidden hatch; it was invisible when viewed from ground level but here, close up, he could just see the hatch outline. It had been deep-filled, repainted, basically resealed for all eternity. Those sneaky bastards.

Once he pressed upward with minimal force, a four-foot square section of ceiling slowly, smoothly, and silently descended on interlocking metal piston rods. In the process, it knocked Fido out of the way, coming to rest on the now large pool of yellow fluid. Simultaneously, a sturdy aluminium steel loft ladder unfurled, leading into the unknown darkness of their eternal hope.

With his pistol drawn, and very tentatively, Fido ascended the ladder. He didn't want Chris injured in the event it was booby-trapped. He still had a job to do. He also didn't want him to see what remained of his girls, especially if the old hag in the cellar was anything to go by. He had been constantly checking for booby traps. For all their shared experiences in the last eight weeks and everything they had been through, this massive life-altering effort had taught him well. The very last thing he wanted was to contribute to any harm to the Beem family. He hoped and prayed. The old saying, *there are no atheists in the trenches*, was never truer when it came to having someone else's life in your hands. So he meant it when he asked God for Chris' family to be safe, to be here in the rafters of this loft because if they were not, they would never be found.

Once on the final rung of the ladder, slowly, cautiously, and with purpose, he entered into a pitch-black loft conversion. It was very apparent it had been recently converted into a sound-proofed holding cell. He could see the floor had been raised two feet away from the original loft flooring. There was a self-contained steel box within the room. It had a steel locking door containing a 12-inch built-in porthole, the box's only source of light. No sound, no matter how loud, would be heard in the room below. It was as clever as it was sickening. Using their high-powered, industrial-strength torches with a remote standalone halogen lamp, the room was quickly fully illuminated. The floodlighting revealed no boobytraps or spiders' webs, which told you this hideous conversion had only been finished in the last few days.

Chris could contain himself no longer and raced up the ladder, charging past Fido with no apology and over to the box. He looked through the porthole. The inside was illuminated by a single candle, its flickering bright blue and orange flame an indicator that the air in the box was slowly depleting.

There, in the far corner, he could just make out the hunched-over forms of Sophie and Tilly. They were huddled together on a clean mattress, in this sound-proof tomb with its own en suite facilities. His heart was full to bursting and the tears streamed down his cheeks. He couldn't stop them, even if he had wanted to. Sophie and Tilly were sitting very still, shocked, stunned, starved, cut and bruised, but very much alive. Just.

The only object between him and redemption for all he had done (the cause and the effect of his greed; was it greed or was it love?) was this massive steel door, which was well and truly locked. It just would not budge. As he looked into the box, he could see the candle flicker, flutter and falter as the oxygen ran out. He didn't know the cubic capacity of the box but he knew they had only minutes left. How much oxygen remained inside, he didn't know. What he did know was he could not come all this way, do all he had done, just to watch his girls die in a steel box, through a 12-inch triple-glazed porthole.

Fido pushed him roughly to one side, making no apology, because he was armed with a heavy-duty portable, propane gas blowtorch, and immediately set about burning out the security lock. At that moment, the candle inside did not have enough oxygen to sustain it. It spluttered and went out, leaving a small smoking ember on the wick, leaving Sophie and Matilda alone in the dark to take their own last wisps of breath.

"Come on, come on, hurry up," screamed Chris, as if Fido was taking it at a leisurely pace. He just couldn't help himself; the fear and frustration were bubbling over and he was losing control. SK would have been able to calm him. Bloody hell, this was just the final straw.

Fido finally, and with great relief, hammered the six-inch steel lock out of position and the door slowly swung open.

Chris raced in and virtually dived on his girls, checking their breathing and pulses. Although weak, they were present, but as the air thickened with a rich balance of nitrogen and oxygen, so did the blood racing around their fatigued, emaciated bodies. Their pulses grew stronger, and their breathing strengthened and steadied. Finally, Sophie opened her tears-stained sunken eyes and tried a small smile, before passing out through the effort.

Tilly was sitting up with the aid of Fido by the time Sophie came around fully. No Nickname had dashed off to get an oxygen cylinder which they were now sharing, drinking in the life which flowed from it.

All Sophie could say through dry, cracked lips and with a croaky little whisper of a voice was, "Why?"

All Chris could do was cry and hug, and hug and cry. He had made it, just in time. They were at last safe.

Why? He knew this was the ultimate question and one with an exceptionally long answer. One he was going to be happy to tell, in all its self-incriminating detail. There would never be a secret or unspoken word in this family ever again, he promised them both, right there and then.

Much later, he would learn his good fortune at seeing the drip, drip, drip, dripping, was nothing more than a freak accident. Tilly had 'kicked the bucket', quite literally – the single bucket in their own en suite bathroom facilities. MB had deliberately left it full so its foul-smelling contents would add to the abject horror of the situation. There would be no getting away from the invasive stench – how she loved her mind games, something she had taken great pleasure in over the last eight weeks. She had warned them that if they spilt the bucket, she would remove the rest of Sophie's digits, leaving them in fear of spilling even a single drop. Their combined, by now totally dehydrated, buttermilk yellow urine, had found the route of least resistance. It had found its way through a bolt hole in the floor of the box, then the joins of the artificial floor, and finally, slowly around the joists in the loft. That sweet trickle of natural body fluid had shown Chris the way, the way to salvation, the way back, and the way forward.

Epilogue

Beem lay hot, sweaty, hungry, and motionless, looking through the sights of a standard-issue, bolt-action M40 sniper rifle, complete with its standard-issue Schmidt & Bender PM II 3-12x50 scout sniper day scope. It already had a hand-made 610 mm round chamber, giving it a maximum range of 1000 yards or 914.4 metres, if you prefer.

At the other end of 876.3 metres was Lucia Maria Domingo, who was being secretly observed, as she had been daily for the last three weeks. Today, it seemed, was going to be the day. Perfect for it in every way: perfect weather and perfect vantage point. All the training had paid off. Perfect.

Today, the madness which had started so long ago was going to end. It had to. The old nightmare was once again rearing its ugly head. The intelligence reports showed her erratic behaviour and unpredictable movements had picked up the pace, as they edged closer to the fortieth anniversary. The threat was once again going to explode into their now settled life, a life which would never again be taken for granted by any member of the Beem family.

A nightmare that they had only just endured. Never again would such a happy family be torn apart. They had worked too hard on repairing the damage done by Lucia's deep-seated hate, hate of everything which had cruelly snatched away her life at 2,600 feet per second.

Hate, it seemed, could not be left to chance. Hate devoured

all the love. It sucked the oxygen out of entire families, laying waste to fragile lives. They would not survive the second tsunami of this hate and destruction; they had barely survived the first.

In the immediate aftermath of the life-changing events of 2012, the whole sorry tale had been pieced together and the answers came in graphic detail. That detailed report had been compiled and updated over the last ten years, painting a horrific picture. It had been read and reread; it was now so well-known it was burned into the memory of all who had read it. It was almost too horrible to recall but it was important to be reminded of why it had come to this.

It had all started in 1982 with the lawful execution of Argentinean Generalissimo Leopoldo Domingo, in defence of the realm and the people of the Falkland Islands, effectively ending the Falklands war. However, at that moment, a chain of unforeseen future events had been set off, creating a trail of destruction which had been almost unstoppable. It created its own energy, its own perpetual motion. Each new event, despite the passage of time, had started the next equally destructive event – a chain reaction.

In 1982, the first event in the chain was the justified execution of the General which had led to the mass mutiny of his forces, including the elite 601 Intelligence Battalion death squad commanders. They, in turn, had taken out their anger and shame of losing on an already pregnant 14-year-old – the General's beautiful daughter, Lucia. The brutal rape and barbaric beatings had only stopped when the inevitable disfigurement was too much to stomach, but Lucia survived and so had the baby. A baby which she had known she was carrying, one conceived in love but born into hate.

In 1983, Lucia had hidden away with her newborn daughter,

Catalina Marie Domingo, in the General's magnificent hillside compound in the foothills of Argentina, on the border with Chile. Supported by a handful of the most loyal servants, rearing her child, even in that opulence and plundered wealth, still had not done anything to soften her heart. It had done nothing to relieve her pain. Her unnaturally deep anger and hatred had grown. Day upon day, her maternal love for her daughter diminished and turned to dust.

Catalina was not just her daughter; she was also the General's.

Love had been replaced with a loathing, kindness with hate, a hatred that no normal mother should ever feel. It was only the thought of vengeance which was keeping her alive. Her father's loving touch and gentle caresses were now a sweet, but distant memory, replaced by thoughts of bloody retribution.

It emerged that the deep-seated, all-consuming guilt which Lucia wore like a crown of thorns was born out of hatred for her own daughter. Never once trying to check or control this abhorrent evil seeping from deep within, she had let it warm and comfort her, let it control her emotions and all her subsequent actions. She never once tried to stop herself from beating or torturing Catalina, along with her wetnurse, Juanita.

Lucia's grip on reality had slipped away more often as the years passed. She had spiralled into a form of madness, manifesting in uncontrollable, near-daily, virtually murderous rages. She decided to rid herself of Catalina while her moral compass still held some sway on her actions. She decided to send her unloved, unwanted, and by now totally despised child away to boarding school.

She had found a good school. Good because it was to provide a high educational standard; good because it was far away from her; good because it was away from all the ills of this world; and good because her enemies, real or imagined, would not look in a small, quiet, but safe city in the distant land of her enemies. No one was able to freely travel to the United Kingdom, to a place called Lincoln.

The report contained a detailed account which told of how Catalina had, despite being a shy child, started to blossom over the years in the clean freshness of this historic jewel.

She would write home regularly with tales of learnings learnt, sports excelled at, coastal walks walked, and theatre visits visited. Life was good, life was full of wonders. The letters told of school friends growing into young, confident, beautiful ladies. The letters were full of life, love of inconsequential interactions, of ships which passed in the night. They contained snippets of information. Some praised a young, acclaimed academic called Brumby-Smith. She had shown Catalina what it was like to feel love. Evidently, she had taken her under her wing, was particularly kind and attentive to her every need, had taken her places far and wide, broadened her horizons, opened her mind to new adventures, and strengthened her worldly experiences through her more mature friends.

From these letters, Lucia had gleaned some small comfort, some hope, when her underlying anger permitted, for at least her own ruined life had produced a beautiful young lady both inside and out. She would go on to do all the things that Lucia had dreamt of as a small child.

Catalina would have the wealth of generations behind her to make those dreams come true.

The letters had abruptly stopped arriving, and despite her initial hatred of Catalina in the early years, the affectionate nature of them had, by now, removed most of the rough bark and smoothed some of Lucia's sharp edges.

Lucia's anger grew once more. She felt she was losing everything all over again and she did not want to lose that spark of love, that ember of life.

After six months had passed, she paid handsomely for a private company to confidentially investigate.

In 1998, Lucia attended a meeting in London with the chief investigator, who did not want to share the report in writing. It soon became apparent why.

Lucia had only recognised her dead daughter because she had taken to carrying a school photo in her Gucci purse. She had forced herself to watch, over and over, the multiple rapes and eventual 'thrill' killing, all captured in glorious 64-bit high definition and available to download for an insignificant $1000 – it was what is known in certain circles as a snuff video.

The report went on to share details of the paedophile ring who were solely responsible for the abuse and death of Catalina. All of them made up 'The List'. A list that had Brumby-Smith on it.

At that moment, Lucia knew she wanted to exact revenge her own way, not by the law of the land. That way would be too soft to be called justice, too soft to be called revenge.

The private investigators had also been tasked to find the name of the soldier who had killed her beloved father, and despite it being a wholly legitimate operation, she still called Captain (Laser) Christopher Beem the murdering *bastardo*.

The private investigators had completed a deep dive, a very deep dive. The report spelt out, in detail, the Beem family history, lock stock and barrel. How he had gone on to secure himself a nice comfortable life with a beautiful wife, Sophie, and gorgeous daughter, Matilda, and with an unforeseen twist of fate, had also lived his tranquil life in Lincoln.

Lucia had gone back home to lick her wounds, to plan a vengeance, one which was more suited to her style.

Revenge for the General's murder; revenge for her shattered life; revenge for the disfigurement which had kept her a prisoner in a cage, albeit a gilded one; revenge for the death of her own beautiful daughter; revenge for abruptly taking away her only spark of love and her father's last gift to her.

All that vengeance had been solely focused on the man who, Lucia wholly believed with all her being, had conceivably started her whole living nightmare.

She had a fire in her blood and hate in her heart; she lived only for bloody retribution.

Lucia had used her considerable resources and unlimited free time. She had spent the intervening fourteen years compiling all the required details to generate a foolproof plan, a doubly delicious plan. One which combined vengeance for the murder of Catalina, together with retribution for the murder of her beloved god of a father, giving her a full circle, neat and tidy, poetic revenge.

Then, in 2012, Lucia, with the help of her Bosnian veterans, had nearly succeeded in her murderous plan. She had almost managed to have the whole paedophile ring killed, nearly achieved her whole catastrophic goal, which included consigning the Beem family to history. Their cage was not gilded. It was, however, near perfect, hidden so well. It had only been luck which had intervened and saved them all.

In her fractured mind, the actual dates had become the catalyst for all her actions. It had all started with her hero, the General, justifiably invading the Falkland Islands on 2 April 1982, to regain control of the Malvinas, rightfully Argentina's sovereignty lands. Then, being murdered on 14 June 1982, right there in front of her pretty little innocent eyes. So, these were the very trigger dates spiralling Lucia into madness.

That's exactly what had happened back in 2012, and that was what was happening again right here, right now, a decade later.

The raw power of the emotions that the story told had clearly been the driving force for Lucia's actions. Hate was the only thing keeping her alive. She had sworn bloody vengeance for the death of her beloved father, and the death of his daughter, her daughter, at the hands of those sick paedophiles. It would never simply just go away. Time would not heal such deep wounds, not for as long as Lucia lived. The threat she posed was real; the storm was coming.

Matilda knew these now-infamous milestone dates. Just a ten-week period, nearly forty years ago, had galvanised Lucia's resolve; everything was set for one final throw of the dice. Lucia had everything in place and was all set to go after Matilda's family once more, but only if she did not end this right here, right now.

Matilda's preparations were now complete, all the known and some unknown factors considered. A fresh bandana kept the sweat out of her eyes and she kissed, for luck, the 24ct gold cross, along with her mother's engagement ring and wedding band set, held together on an 18ct gold belcher chain around her neck. She stowed these away while she adjusted her position, confident her dad's old ghillie suit was, at 876.3 metres, keeping her out of sight. This was all part of her routine to get her into the zone.

She quietly unloaded and cleaned the round, knowing dust and humidity affected the round's trajectory. She silently rechambered it; she would only need the one. Physically controlling the movement of her oxygen-depleted lungs with slow, even breaths, she gently applied pressure, taking up the first stage of the trigger. Then, at the exact right moment, timing it to coincide with the apex of the release of her hot silent breath, she gently squeezed the trigger with just the right amount of kinetic energy. Simultaneously, she leaned into the stock slightly, to control the recoil. Finally, completing the action, she fired at 2,600 feet per second.